Ballad of Favour

A small child's cry of fear is the beginning of a new adventure for Rose Wood, chosen messenger of Favour, the magical Great Grey Horse.

What does it mean? Rose knows that when the horse carries her into different scenes and different times, she is supposed to find clues there.

'The child might have been abandoned – it might have been hurt,' she tells her friend Mr Vingo. 'But I don't know who it was or where it was or when it was.'

'Trust the horse,' says Mr Vingo. 'He'll show you.'

Centuries ago the horse belonged to the repulsive Lord of the Moor, and found fame in his heroic race to save a village. Now he lives on to fight against evil and despair.

As his messenger, Rose must fly with him to a small, decrepit, back street, and learn what makes the child cry so pitifully. The clues are there – a railway line, a fun fair, a TV programme, a birthday – but how do they fit together? Rose must find the solution before it is too late.

This is the second book about Rose and the Great Grey Horse. The first book, THE MESSENGER, tells of Rose's early encounters with Favour, and her struggle to rid the house next door of a tragic haunting.

About the author

MONICA DICKENS, a great-granddaughter of Charles Dickens, went to St. Paul's School for Girls, in London, where she won two scholarships but was expelled for feeding her school hat to the family dog.

Since then she has become famous all over the world for her bestselling books. As well as nearly thirty adult titles, she has written a number of stories for children, including the *Follyfoot* books (which were made into a very successful TV series) and four *World's End* titles.

Many of her books reflect her lifetime love of animals, especially horses – in fact, animals are such a part of her life that she finds it hard to keep them out of her stories. In the *Messenger* series she writes about the kind of horse one might dream about: wild, majestic and beautiful.

Monica has two grown-up daughters, a horse called Robin, two dogs, Mollie and Rosie, and an assortment of cats.

Monica Dickens

Ballad of Favour

Illustrations by
Glynis Overton

Armada

Ballad of Favour was first published in the U.K. in 1985
in hardback by William Collins Sons & Co. Ltd.,
and in paperback in Armada,
by Fontana Paperbacks, 8 Grafton Street, London W1X 3LA.

Printed and bound in Great Britain by
Anchor Brendon Ltd, Tiptree, Essex

CHAPTER ONE

By late September, the Wood Briar Hotel was only half full.

Rose, who lived and worked there, had loved the busy summer, with all the rooms in the hotel and its annexe house taken, but autumn was a good time too, with less work and more time for herself when she came home from school.

Soft misty days were perfect for riding, and the sea was still just warm enough to swim when the sun was out. Weekenders came, and a few retired people pottered about the hotel, giving no trouble, taking walks, reading on the verandah in the low golden sunshine.

One-nighters on car trips were more relaxed, and often stayed an extra night. Salesmen on the road were still cheery before the winter wore them out. Jake and Julie, two of Rose's favourite guests, still came from the city for a night or two. Her friend Ben would come with his family when he had a weekend off from school. The elusive Mr Vingo, who lived in the round turret bedroom with his little yellow upright piano, would probably turn up again soon from one of his mysterious disappearances.

Although he and Rose were close friends, and shared the colossal secret about the legendary Great Grey Horse, he would never tell her where he had been, or why. He would leave without warning and then just reappear, bulky and out of breath, and say something like, 'Yes, thank you, I will have tea and two thin slices of that good pound cake,' as if he had never been away.

The small seaside hotel stood across the road from low sand dunes and a long curved beach; a gabled, turreted old house which had been built a century ago by someone with a taste for stained glass windows and odd bulges and

5

balconies. Next to it stood a smaller, red brick house that was used as an annexe to the hotel, with extra bedrooms and a lounge.

When Rose's parents, Philip and Mollie Wood, bought the hotel four years ago, it was called with mournful grandeur, 'The Cavendish'. It had been shabby and gloomy, with terrible food and bad service. Now it was all white paint and bright rugs and curtains, with real flowers on the dining-room tables instead of dusty plastic ones, and well-fed guests who were made to feel at home. The hotel had been rechristened 'Wood Briar', because the girl who lived there was called Rose Wood.

Rose was thirteen. She was energetic and practical, and she helped the staff with all the jobs in the bedrooms and the kitchen and dining-room.

'If you can call it help,' Mrs Ardis said in one of her many different voices, a hoity toity one designed to show that she had known a much better life than being a chambermaid.

Making beds with her, Rose had flung down a pillow and flown to the window at a shout from below. Abigail on her dun pony – Abigail was back! She pulled in her head and said, 'Won't be a sec.'

'I know your "secs".' Mrs Ardis bent with a groan to pick up the pillow, and punched it as if she would like to do the same to Rose.

But Rose was gone, scooting along the twisting corridor, sliding down the bannisters, jumping far out into the hall and skidding on a rug, to the outrage of old Mrs Plummer who was sitting behind a large fern waiting for her taxi to take her to the hairdresser, to have her stiff grey sausage curls dyed blue. Rose dashed through the kitchen where Hilda was stringing late beans and reading the paper with her one good eye, and outside to where Abigail sat gracefully on her pony on the back lawn.

'Where you *been*?' They always said that to each other, whether they had been apart for months, or only days or hours.

6

'Well, you know. In Chicago.' Abigail was American. 'But Dad's back here now at the engineering plant, so we've opened up the farmhouse. Where you bin?'

'Here.' Rose grinned, and rolled the sleeves of her overall higher. 'Working.'

'So what's new?' Abigial always said that. She said, 'What's noo?'

'Nothing much.' Rose wanted to say, 'Lots,' but she couldn't tell Abigail about the enormous and splendid adventure that had come into her life when she was chosen as a messenger of Favour, the Great Grey Horse, in his fight against the sad and bad things of the world. So she laughed and said, 'Mrs Ardis gave in her notice this morning.' This was a weekly ritual, sometimes daily, if things were too hectic in the summer, or too boring in the winter. 'Jake and Julie's dog dug up the bulbs my mother planted. Dilys's new boy friend broke her heart, and she broke five sherry glasses. A man called Robert McRobert did four crossword puzzles and two jigsaws before lunch on a rainy day. Hilda used coffee syrup instead of gravy browning . . .'

'So what else is new?' Abigail's long chestnut hair was pulled tightly into a plait down her back, stretching the corners of her lively eyes. She had a pointed face, like an elf.

'I don't know what's *new*.' Rose's father had come out of the shed that was his summer workshop behind the hotel, where he tested products for a magazine that told people what to buy. 'But what's old is that I've asked you before not to ride that damn horse on my lawn.'

'It's a pony, Dad,' Rose said bluntly, and Abigail explained, 'He doesn't have any shoes. He's been out to grass all summer.'

'That's not the point.' Philip Wood was treading back a small piece of turf raised by the pony's hoof, with as much fuss as if it had been made by a bulldozer.

'Hi, Mr Wood,' Abigail said charmingly. 'It's so good to see you again.'

'Good to see you.' Rose's father nodded ungraciously and went on into the hotel.

7

Rose wished he could be like Abigail's father, who welcomed you as if you were the one person in the world he'd been wanting to see, but Abigail said cheerfully, 'He's neat, your Dad. Leaves you guessing.'

Above them, Mrs Ardis pushed her head of wild brindle hair out of a bedroom window and called in one of her coarser voices, 'It's now or never, Rose!'

If that was why the pony flung up his head from the grass and jumped sideways, why was he afterwards still tense and quivering, flicking his short Arab ears back and forth, staring away from the hotel towards the wood?

'Cool it, you jerk.'

Abigail could not hear anything. Only Rose heard it, beyond the wood on the turf of the moor, the drumbeat of galloping hoofs. Into her head came the first rising notes of the horse's strange tune, dropping into the low, thrilling staccato of a snort blown into the wind.

She had not seen him for so long, she was afraid she had lost him, but now she knew that he had never been far away from her, the challenging spirit of the Great Grey Horse that hovered always at the edge of her dreams.

Rose's mother was delighted to see Abigail again. Mollie Wood was a young, pretty woman with curly gold hair which she had not passed on to Rose, whose hair was straight and neither blonde nor brown. The hotel was Mollie's joy and pride. She did everything she could to make the guests happy and comfortable – far too much, according to her husband, to whom guests were customers, who shouldn't get more than they paid for. One of the reasons she liked Abigail was that Rose's American friend loved the Wood Briar Hotel as much as Rose and Mollie did.

'Just the woman I've been hoping to see!'

Abigail grinned at Mollie's greeting. 'Me too, Mrs Wood. The hotel looks swell. Can I come and help Rose some time?'

'This evening, if you like. We're going to be busy. You can help Rose to serve dinners.'

Abigail thought it was the finest thing in the world, and was constantly nagging her parents to buy a hotel in Chicago. When she came back, she tied on one of Rose's blue check aprons, which looked instantly elegant on her, while on Rose it just looked like a short blue check apron, and helped to lay the tables. After the usual argument about whether the pudding spoon went beside the knife or above it, she and Rose went out into the fine September rain to pick some chrysanthemums from the garden of the annexe house next door.

'There used to be ghosts in this house, you know.' Everyone had thought that was Rose's imagination, but Abigail believed it.

'Oh, gee.'

'They've gone now.'

'Where?'

'Who knows? Wherever ghosts go when they've been released from haunting.'

'Darn it,' Abigail said. 'You might have kept them for me.'

'You like ghosts, madam?' a man's voice asked from the other side of the garden wall, as if he were selling ghosts in a department store.

Rose stood up. Of course. Mr Vingo usually came back in this kind of weather. He liked the rain.

'Favour is back,' she muttered quickly, to let him know without Abigail hearing. He nodded and winked, one large smooth upper lid descending like the back of a spoon under the turned up brim of his rain hat.

'And so is – so is Abigail.' Rose had been longing to introduce her two best friends. Now she was nervous. Would they like each other? She had told Mr Vingo about Abigail, and written to Abigail about Mr Vingo. Would her enthusiastic descriptions fit at all? 'Abigail Drew. Mr R. V. Vingo.' That was his name in the hotel register. Sometimes

9

'You like ghosts, madam . . ?'

Mollie wrote up his bill as Harvey Vingo. It didn't seem to matter.

Mr Vingo looked shy. If Rose had been Abigail, she would have been shy too, but Abigail never seemed to bother with things like shyness and doubt. She stood up, holding a bunch of red and gold flowers, with Mollie's yellow oilskin jacket round her shoulders and her eyes shining, and said, 'You must be the gentleman with the piano.'

'Indeed.' Mr Vingo's thick eyebrows smoothed out and one of his great baggy smiles crumpled the flesh of his broad pale face. 'And you must be the lady with the flute.'

How did he know? Rose could not have told him, since Abigail had only told her today. But Mr Vingo knew a lot of things, or else he was a lucky guesser.

'I'm only just learning to play the flute,' Abigail said.

'Well, I'm really only learning to play the piano,' Mr Vingo said, although he was a composer, and could produce captivating music from his narrow marmalade piano that stood against the curving wall of his turret room. 'The piano and the flute go well together. We must learn a duet.'

'Hey, yeah.' Abigail reached across the wall and gave him a wet bronze chrysanthemum.

CHAPTER TWO

The hotel dining-room was full for dinner. Mollie's reputation for good food had spread, and people from the nearby village of Newcome Hollow and the town of Newcome two miles away liked to come out at night, especially when it was raining. Bad weather outside seemed to turn their thoughts inward to their stomachs.

Mr Vingo had to share his small corner table with a new guest, a youngish woman called Miss Elisabeth Engel, who had long, ash-coloured hair wound round her head, and a sad, tired face. She was recuperating from a nervous breakdown, according to the gossip of the staff, who always knew everything about every new guest before they had been in the hotel an hour.

Mr Vingo managed to make her smile, and although she had told Rose at the beginning that she only wanted celery soup, she ate a little of the chicken and Mollie's bread and butter pudding, and told Abigail at the end of the meal that she was glad she had come to Wood Briar.

'Oh, gee,' Abigail said.

'Girl.' Mrs Plummer could not distinguish between Abigail and Rose, although Abigail was tall for her age and slender, and Rose was short and rather stocky. 'This table is not laid correctly.'

'American style, ma'am,' Abigail said.

'It's not what I'm used to.' Mrs Plummer picked up the spoon and dipped it in her water glass and polished it on her napkin, holding it high, so everyone could see, and then dropped the napkin on the floor and asked for a new one, and another glass of water.

The waitress Gloria, brisk and violent, went fuming into the pantry where Mollie was dishing up. Rose and Abigail had to hold in their giggles until they could carry them out with their trays to the kitchen and dump the giggles on each other.

When they had cleared the tables and eaten their own supper of good things Mollie had held back for them, Abigail's mother fetched her, and Rose went looking for Mr Vingo.

He was not in his room. The windows were not making their semicircular pattern of lighted oblongs on the grass below the turret. He was not in the upstairs lounge or in the nook by the hall fireplace or on the verandah, where he sometimes sat in the dark, listening to the endless sound of the sea beyond the dunes, which you could not hear in the daytime, unless there was a storm.

She found him in the annexe lounge, sitting with the French windows open on to the ripe damp autumn smells of the orchard.

'What now?' Rose kicked off her shoes and sat on the sill of the doorway with her bare feet getting gently wet on the step outside.

'What now, messenger? Another job for you, it seems.'

'I was afraid Favour was finished with me.'

'Because he lets you catch up with your life between jobs? He won't finish with you as long as you do the work right, and in secret. You haven't told your – ah – your, ah–' he was short of breath, because he had eaten a large meal and a handful of Mr Barrett's marzipans. 'Your transatlantic –'

'Abigail? No. I wish I could. She'd die. It's funny,' Rose said. 'She keeps telling me about all the exciting things going on in Chicago, and she thinks I'm just the same old Rose who never goes anywhere or does anything except go to school and help run Wood Briar. Ha!' She let a shout of laughter out into the night. 'If she only knew.'

When Rose became thirteen, the mystical grey horse Favour had called her to come to him, because she was now travelling through the special age between childhood and growing up, when fantasy can become reality, and you are sensitive enough to see things unseen by other people, and strong and brave enough for adventure.

The horse had been coming and going on the earth for centuries, long after he was supposed to have died. His crusading mission was to protect the innocent from evil and disaster and misery. He needed human beings to help him, and he chose them from among these special people. He had chosen Rose.

'Perhaps I shall play Abigail some of my music for *The Ballad of the Great Grey Horse*, Mr Vingo said, tapping his knee as he thought about the music. 'And I shall tell her, "Miss Abigail," I shall say, "this is the legend of how Favour, the favourite horse of the dreaded Lord, galloped against the flood to save the valley people." Even though she can't know where you fit in.'

Messengers must never tell anybody about the horse, or where he had taken them to do his work. Mr Vingo knew, because he had once been a messenger too, countless years ago when he was Rose's age.

'She'll like the part about the wicked Lord of the Moor and his beastly soldiers,' Rose said. 'She loves horror stories. Oh . . .' She hugged her knees and frowned out at the wet apples glistening in the grass in the light from the house. 'I hope I don't have to fight my way through them again. They terrify me.'

'But to reach the horse, there must be struggle,' Mr Vingo said behind her. 'And terror too, Rose, if need be. If it was easy to be a messenger, Rose of all Roses, where would be the glory?'

'Where will he take me?' Excitement had fired up in Rose. She pulled in her feet and got up to pace the carpet of the lounge. 'Will he take me back into the past, or into the future? How will I know what I have to do?'

'You'll know.' Mr Vingo followed her pacing with his eyes, without turning his head.

'Will you help me?'

His answer was lost in a flash of white light and a

14

deafening crack of thunder that exploded together over the house. In the glare of the lightning's after-image, Rose saw the horse standing in front of the apple trees, his beautiful head flung up and his ears straining forward, his luminous grey eyes fixed on her. Then it was all black outside and he was gone, and she held herself tightly with her arms crossed, hugging the electric excitement.

'Rose of all Roses.' Mr Vingo quoted softly behind her from the old poem that he liked to weave around her name. 'Rose of all the World.'

CHAPTER THREE

Another thing that qualified Rose to be one of Favour's messengers was that she truly loved and understood horses.

She was a terrible rider, who would never be good enough to perform at horse shows or events, but she did not love horses because of how fast they could race or how high they could jump, or how many rosettes they could win. She loved them for being horses, just as they were, not only the proud, expensive ones, but the clumsy, ugly ones too. Perhaps these even more so, because most horsy people didn't appreciate them.

At the stables on the edge of the moor where she took riding lessons with some of the money she earned at the hotel, she almost always rode the same pale, pink-eyed horse, Moonlight; partly because she wasn't good enough for the better ones, partly because she and Moonlight needed each other.

Joyce, who ran the stable with her mother, complained that he cantered as if he had five legs. When he stumbled or crashed through a small jump instead of over it, she would call him Mule, and threaten to send him to the sausage factory.

He was tall and bony, with a stained, cream-coloured coat, big sloppy feet and a spine too long for his front and back ends to communicate to each other what they were doing.

But he and Rose communicated a lot of things to each other, and today as she brushed him down after a ride on the moor with Abigail and a group from the stable, she told him how she had seen the grey horse in the lightning, and how she believed that he was ready to take her on another journey. Today? Tomorrow? She shared her excitement with Moonlight, and her secrets. He was her four-legged version of Mr Vingo.

'You croon to that old mule as if he was a baby.' Joyce looked over the loosebox door. 'I don't know what he'll do when you graduate to better things. You looked pretty good today, trotting along beside your friend on that snappy dun pony of hers. I may let you have a go on Sheba next time.'

'*Could* I?' Rose was torn between loyalty to Moonlight and the chance to ride the bay mare Sheba, who was trained for the show ring and would break into a smooth canter if you only thought about it.

'We'll see.' Joyce loved the power of keeping you in suspense. 'Come on, girl, put some elbow grease into it. *Lean* on the brush. He's not made of china.'

Rose leaned. Moonlight staggered.

Abigail had ridden her pony home. Rose followed her on the bicycle that was called Old Paint, because it was old and repainted, and small enough for her to swerve around stones and puddles as if she were neck-reining a Western cow pony. She was saving her work money to buy a new one, but she would miss this old faithful friend when it was gone.

'How come you don't ask Joyce to give you a better horse?' Abigail asked, when Rose got to the farm.

'Well, she might. She even said so. But –' she had not yet resolved the conflict between loyalty and ambition – 'I don't think I'm ready for something like Sheba.'

'Baloney. You could ride O.K. on a better horse.' Abigail was leading her dun pony Crackers to turn him out in the field. 'Here, get on Crackers and have a go around the yard.'

'Bareback?'

Moonlight's spine was a bony ridge. Rose had never ridden bareback, except during her dream-like gallops with the grey horse Favour, and that was more like flying.

'Sure, he's used to it.'

'In a halter?'

'Come on, Rose, don't be chicken. Here, stand close up to him and bend your leg back.'

17

Abigail could leap on to the pony's back with ease, but Rose had to be hoisted and boosted.

'Trot around the yard.' Abigail gave her the halter rope. Rose tried to hold on to the pony's mane, which was very thin and short, so that Abigail could plait it for the shows she would go to this autumn.

'Ter-rot!' Abigail imitated Joyce's roar. 'C'mon there, get em going, you bunch of layabouts – ter-*rot*, I said!'

But the yard was cluttered with various farm things, and as Rose kicked the pony too heartily, he leaped forward, and a cat shot out from under a wheelbarrow, and he jumped sideways and Rose fell neatly off on to a pile of wet feed sacks.

'New way of dismounting?'

What was so great about Abigail was that she could always make a joke about whatever happened. They turned the pony out with his mate, a chestnut called Cheese, and watched him roll, teetering on the black stripe that ran down his back, until he finally thumped over on the other side with a satisfied grunt. Then Abigail put her arm through Rose's and said, 'Come on up to the hay loft and I'll show you my new toy.'

It was a real farmhouse where Abigail lived, with a barn and cart sheds, and two old-fashioned looseboxes with low thatched roofs built against the side of the barn. The land was let to a tenant farmer, and his wife looked after the house when the Drews were in America.

The hay loft over one end of the barn was Rose and Abigail's favourite place. They slept there sometimes, instead of in Abigail's comfortable bedroom which had its own bathroom and patchwork quilts on the beds. They were made by Abigail's mother's grandmother years ago out of pieces left over from the dresses and shirts and tablecloths she had sewn for her family out on the Western frontier.

Abigail's flute was in its case on a ledge among the beams of the loft, a lovely slender instrument like a shepherd's pipe.

'I've been practising up here, because my dad laughs at me if I play in the house. He says it sounds like cats on the backyard fence.'

'Don't you mind?'

'Nah, it's just a joke.'

'When my father laughs at me,' Rose said with difficulty, because even with Abigail she found it hard to talk about inner things, 'it isn't funny. It hurts. When I was a silly little kid, I used to go away and cry and tell myself I hated him. But I don't hate him. I want to like him. But we fight.'

As she grew into her teens, she had become more at odds with her father. Even with her bright, companionable mother, whose jokes really were funny, Rose would sometimes storm and weep and argue, and about one in four family meals ended up with her crashing her chair backwards and running out of the room.

'Well, you gotta understand.' Abigail lay back luxuriously into a broken hay bale. 'Adults have problems. You gotta make allowances.'

'That's what my father says about teenagers. When I get really angry with him, and start shouting and kicking the furniture, he tells me it's adolescence, and I'll grow out of it one day. Why is that so infuriating?'

'Because they miss the point,' Abigail said. 'It's not what's going to happen one day that matters. It's what's happening now.'

'And in any case.' Rose was sitting up, looking out of the open window to the marvellous view of a sloping green field with two ponies in it, a stand of dark trees along the top edge, and beyond them the blurred pastel colours of the distant moorland hills. 'I don't know that I want to grow out of being this age.'

'But poor old Rose, you gotta grow up and have adventures.'

'I'm having them.' Rose smiled to herself out of the window.

'Nah, I mean the real adventures of life. You can't just go on being old Rose that nothing ever happens to. Here, I'll play you a tune to call you into life.'

She sat up and put the long slim flute sideways to her lips

19

and began to play, rather slowly, but with only a few mistakes.

O Danny boy . . . the pipes, the pipes are calling . . .

She sat in the hay with her lips pursed sweetly to the mouthpiece of the flute, her fingers moving gracefully on the keys on top of it, her eyes shut, because she was concentrating.

She did not know it, but she really was calling Rose to the adventures of her life. Through the haunting tune, *The summer's gone, and all the roses falling . . .*, the alluring music that called Rose to the grey horse began to rise and drown out the notes of 'Danny Boy'.

Rose had to get up and, without an explanation, jump down from the loft into the straw pile, and take off through the barn door towards the moor.

Usually she went through the wood behind the hotel, across the sheep pasture and out towards the hills on a twisting sheep track that led her to the hidden valley. She did not know if she could find it from this direction, but she just ran, following the tune in her head. Soon, landmarks became familiar, a dead tree pointing like a scarecrow, the rounded masses of the far hills on one side and the triangular hill ahead, and as she came round the corner of an old broken wall, there it was. The huge dark grey rock that stood like a man keeping watch for her.

Beyond it, she plunged into the dense thicket, and pushed through the undergrowth to where the lake called Noah's Bowl should be.

But the lake was not there. Only the thick swirling mist. She knew she had to step through the mist and down, feeling her way, down into the valley that used to be here before the flood filled it up into a lake.

The valley was still here for her, because she was out of the world and out of time now, in a place and time where the horse had his being. Other creatures were here too. She began to sense them, moving around her like shadows in the mist: the hulking shapes of the soldiers, some of them

20

cloaked and hooded in humped masses like the dark rock above, some of them showing glimpses of their faces, a gapped grin of rotten teeth, a smouldering eye, a red wet mouth smiling at her through a tangled beard. She smelled their sweat, the hot scent of their horses, the smoke from their fires. She heard the stamp of a boot on cobbles, an iron chain shaken, the ringing of a hammer on an anvil.

As she groped her way desperately through the weaving mist, using her hands to part it like thick cobwebs, they stayed away from her, the soldiers, but she knew that they were watching her, and her skin crept with fear. She made herself go on, until suddenly she was through the mist, beyond the soldiers, out into the bright sunlight of the valley floor, with the river leaping and turning in sparkling eddies under the old stones of the bridge.

And there above her in a blaze of light as she ran on to the slippery planks of the bridge, the grey horse was poised on his platform of rock, mane and tail swept sideways by the wind that blew down the valley to where the little white fishermen's houses huddled by the sea, his coat glowing and his shining eyes impatient for her to hurry.

She scrambled up the other side of the valley, over the pile of stones and out on to the big rock above and behind him where she could feel his warmth and glowing energy, and make the jump that landed her on his strong, soft back just in time as he leaped up and away into the sunlight.

The speed and rhythm of his flying gallop put her into a kind of trance of joy, through which, echoing faintly at first, then louder, she heard a girl's sharp voice.

'Hurry up, Linda, we're late. Hurry up, can't you?'

The girl was walking fast ahead of Linda, looking over her shoulder with a scowl and a sneer of the lips that distorted her thickly made up face. She called back scornfully, 'You're a dead loss, you are. If the bloomin' strap's broken, take the shoes off and come as nature made you, even if nature made a horrible mistake.'

21

'It's all right, I'm fixing it. Wait for me, Susan – wait!'

Rose was Linda, bending over the strap of her new high-heeled sandal, trying to push it through the stiff buckle, puffing, her heart racing, almost crying because she was enraged with the stupid sandal, and afraid that Susan would run off without her and scoop up the boys and leave her on her own for the evening, as she had done before.

Rose was inside Linda. She could feel her emotions and what it was like to be her, but at the same time she was still Rose and could observe her.

Rose had never worn high heels. When Linda, cursing and snivelling, finally got the strap through the buckle, pulled it tight enough to cut into her instep and stood up and tottered after Susan, it felt odd and insecure, like walking on stilts.

'Wait for me, Suze.'

'That's all I ever do. Sometimes I wonder why I let you come out with me at all.'

'I know. You're nice. I really appreciate it, Suze, I really do.'

Rose didn't like the way Linda toadied to Susan, who was conceited and rather beastly. Linda seemed in some kind of panic to make Susan like her, and Rose could have told her she was going about it all wrong.

When Susan said, 'I had a tough time getting Fred to bring a fellow for you, and this Austin creep who's coming is a totally dim person with spots and boils and only half your height, but it's the best you'll get,' Rose wished Linda would retort, 'Who needs him?' But she knew from past journeys into other people's bodies that she was only a passenger. She could not influence them.

'I'm sure he'll be nice, Suze,' Linda said weakly, although she was in a panic about boys, too.

They were walking through back streets in a town that might be Newcome, or it might not. When Linda's ankle turned in the tottery sandals and she had to stop to rub it, Susan went round a corner, and Linda hobbled to catch her up in a shabby, decaying street that looked as if most of the inhabitants had deserted it.

A row of terrace houses on one side had windows that were broken or boarded up. Planks were nailed across the doors. Front steps were cracked and chipped. Rubbish and old metal were strewn in the weedy gardens between the houses and the dirty pavement.

An open space, part Tarmac and part sour grass where a house had been demolished, had been used as a playground. Cricket stumps were chalked on the end wall among rude messages and crude pictures. The rusted remains of a climbing frame lurched sideways. One end of a see-saw stuck up in the air like a signal for help. The other was hidden in a heap of old newspapers.

Where was this? And *when* was it? Sometimes the horse took Rose into the past, but from the clothes the girls wore and the people they were talking about – singers, rock stars – she must be in her own present time, but in an unknown place.

'Cuba Libre,' Linda said, trying to impress Susan. 'My sister's got their new album.'

'Who cares?' Nothing could impress snooty Susan, with her jeans bleached and shrunk to fit her skinny legs like a second skin, and an odd patch of lurid colour dyed into the front of her spiky hair. 'Those people don't exist. The only one that ever was and ever will be is Bagman, and you know I'd die for him.'

'Oh, I know you would,' Linda agreed, though she didn't care for Bagman and his deafening blasts. 'So would I.'

'He doesn't want creeps like you dying for him.' Susan sneered with her purple upper lip. 'Dying is strictly reserved for those worthy of it.'

Bagman had only screamed his brutal way into the charts in the last two or three weeks, so Rose was right. She had not gone into the past this time.

The high wall of a railway embankment cut off the end of this depressing street. Two or three houses that crouched in the shadow of the wall looked as if people still lived in them. Sad grey washing flapped without spirit in a bare garden on the left. A mangy cat sat pressed against the window in an empty flower box, waiting to be let in. The single house on the right, surrounded by what looked like several lifetimes of junk, was larger but even shabbier. The gate hung on one hinge. Slates had fallen from the roof. Torn curtains sagged at the windows. Missing panes were patched with paper. The paint on the front door was faded and peeling, and a pram without wheels was upside down in front of it. Against the side wall, among overflowing dustbins, an old rusted bicycle leaned with its front wheel turned at an exhausted angle, as if it had breathed its last.

'Charming place,' Susan said with a sniff. 'They'd ought to have condemned it long ago.'

'Perhaps it's the only place the people can find to live?' Linda suggested. 'The housing shortage is wicked.' Her mother worked at the Town Hall, and she knew about these things.

'Don't be soppy. Come *on*, stupid, we're late.'

As they approached the house, Linda and Rose heard behind a curtained window the blare of a pop song.

'At least they got some music, if nothing else.'

They had an unhappy child, too. From the upper floor they heard it crying, a desperate, frightened wail.

'Hang on a minute, Suze.' Linda stopped. 'I don't like the sound of that.' She had several younger brothers and sisters, and she knew one cry from another.

'Oh, shut up. All little kids cry.' Susan took her arm and pulled her roughly forward, but Linda held back.

'No one's doing anything for him.'

'Why should they? Temper, that's all it is.'

'No.' Linda knew. 'It's fear. Suppose they can't hear him 'cos of the noise? Suppose they've left the music on and gone out? Suppose he's all alone? Suppose he's being beaten? There's a lot of that about. We ought to do something. What can we do?'

24

'Nothing.' Susan dragged her past the drunken gate. 'Stop being a rotten do-gooder. It's not our business.'

'I suppose not.' For a moment, Rose had been proud of Linda for resisting, but now she was back under Susan's control, and allowing herself to be pulled into the narrow tunnel that ran under the railway.

'We're late – we're late!' Susan ran ahead, her voice echoing eerily in the sooty brick tunnel. Linda ran after her with her knees bent to stop her ankles turning, in her ears, pursuing her through the dismal, smelly tunnel, the pitiful wails of the child, growing fainter. 'Mumma!' She heard him cry, and choke on a sob.

Rose ran out of the darkness of the tunnel into the sunlight of the moor. There was no Susan. No Linda. No railway wall and no mean streets. The only thing left of the odd, upsetting scene was the sound in her ears of the child's crying. She shook her head, but it was still faintly there, as if it would haunt her for the rest of her days.

When she went back to the Drews' house to get her bicycle, Abigail came out of the back door, looking cross.

'Where you *been*?'

'Sorry I ran off. I just remembered something I had to do.'

'Like what?'

'I – ' It was hateful to have to lie to Abigail, but she could not tell her the truth. 'I found a bird with a dragging wing yesterday. I put him in a bush, and I had to go and see if he's been able to fly away.'

'Just like that? Gee, you are weird. Well – had he?'

'Had he what? Oh yes – yes, he'd gone.'

'Hope he wasn't eaten by an eagle.'

'There aren't any eagles.'

'There are in the States.' When Abigail was put out, she wasn't very logical. 'You ran out on my flute playing. You're worse than my father.'

'It was the tune you played. It – it reminded me of – of the bird, you see.'

25

'Why?'

'The way it goes up, you know, in those rising notes?'

'"Danny Boy" mostly goes down.'

'Not that. The other tune you started to play.'

'What's got into you?' Abigail said, as Rose got on to Old Paint and turned him towards the road. 'I only played "Danny Boy".'

CHAPTER FOUR

What did it mean? Rose knew that when the horse carried her into different scenes and different times, she was supposed to find clues there, which would fit together to show her the final solution.

'In a way,' she told Mr Vingo, when she took his letters up the spiral stair to his room where he was practising, 'Favour is like someone writing a detective story. You get clues, but you don't know what they mean, and he expects you to be as clever as he is.'

'That's why you're chosen.' With his broad bottom spread over the round piano stool, Mr Vingo kept on playing with his back to her. He was practising the merry 'Dancing Song of the Valley People', that he was going to teach Abigail to play with him as a duet.

'I'm not clever,' Rose said, giving his back the dumb stare that she gave teachers at school who asked too much of her.

'Yes, you are. Yes, you aah-haah-haah!' Mr Vingo sang, wagging his head, so that the back of his hair, which always needed cutting, moved over the collar of his grey jacket.

'Can I tell you something?'

'There's no law against it.'

'I got a clue.'

Rose thought he would swing round and look at her, pleased and excited, but he kept playing the same phrase over and over again, tutting and muttering and stabbing at the keys, as if they were trying to escape from the piano.

'A child was crying.'

'Good.'

'It was bad. He might have been abandoned – he might have been hurt.'

'I mean, good that you can do something about it.'

'I don't know how I can. I don't know who it was or where it was or when it was. Some time in the present, but I don't know if it was today, or yesterday, next week, next month. I wish you'd help.'

He swung round then, with his stubby fingers in the air, and saw her pouting.

'But it's you who has to do it, Rose. You know that. Wait. Trust the horse. He'll show you. Believe.'

He swung back to the piano, the rusty screw of the stool shrieking in protest, and she knew he would not turn round again.

One of the letters that had arrived in this morning's post was from the Kelly family, to ask if they could come next weekend. The oldest son Ben was fifteen, and although he sometimes treated Rose like a child when he was being grown up or wanted to tease her, he was Rose's hero, and they were friends.

The Kellys liked to stay in the annexe next door to the hotel. Mollie had converted it from an ordinary house, and decorated it brightly, with a little snack kitchen where guests could make their own breakfast, and sandwiches if they wanted.

A messy family who spilled things in the kitchen and trailed biscuit crumbs everywhere, including the stairs, moved out just before the weekend, and Mollie asked Rose to go in after school and help Mrs Ardis clean up.

Rose was hoovering the big front bedroom for Mr and Mrs Kelly. Running a vacuum cleaner was boring work, but it was one of life's necessitites, and at least it was moronic enough to give the mind a chance to roam free over its own thoughts. As so often now, when her mind was idling, the memory of a small child's crying came back to trouble Rose.

Favour had a reason for taking her into the body of that cowardly toady Linda. She had to experience the shabby street, and had to hear the wailing child. If only Favour could talk to her! But although he was all-wise and immortal, he was still a horse and could not do human things. He knew where trouble was, but he had to use people to put it right.

People like Rose. Rose of all the world . . . to travel anywhere in the world with him, and to any time in history . . .

She saw herself as she had once been as Lilian, in one of the journeys of the first mystery to which the horse had summoned her. She wore a long green dress with lace mittens and a bonnet and coy corkscrew ringlets, a hundred years ago, travelling and observing there within a space of no time in the present, since time was really only a matter of thought, and not a line running backwards and forwards.

'Suck the pattern off the carpet, you will,' Mrs Ardis, coming in with clean sheets, shouted over the motor, 'if you keep running that machine on the same spot. How are we going to get this place cleaned up from those cannibals? You're dreaming, girl, staring out of the window like that.'

But of course Rose was staring. Across the road, in a gap between the swell of two sand dunes, she had seen a flash of movement, the flick of a grey tail, a scudding of sand kicked up, and through the roar of the ageing vacuum cleaner, which was as noisy as a car with a broken exhaust pipe, she clearly heard the flute-like notes of Favour's tune.

When Mrs Ardis had dumped the sheets on the double bed as if they were lead, and plodded out with many sighs, and could be heard treading sufferingly about overhead, Rose left the vacuum cleaner running so Mrs Ardis could hear it, and darted like a swallow out of the front door. She went across the road and over the grassy top of a sand dune, straight on to the back of the grey horse who was waiting there for her, pawing gently at the soft sand.

'Come and change the baby, Carol, there's a love. I'm up to my eyes in suds.'

The woman's voice was hoarse but cheerful. Carol, who

had been upstairs on her bed reading a comic, turned her head towards the stairs and yelled, 'Coming!' but did not move.

Rose was Carol, in a school blouse and skirt, who would have been flat on her back, except that the bed was sagging, not flat. She held the comic up between her face and the damp, flaking ceiling. Her hands were rough, as Rose's were from work, and even dirtier.

The bedroom was small and cold. One pane of the window was stuffed with newspaper. The chest of drawers stood on three legs and a brick. The mirror on the wardrobe door was shattered in a thousand starred cracks, as if a wicked stepmother had looked into it. Clothes of children of various sizes and sexes hung on nails or were strewn on the floor among broken toys. Carol had a bag of toffees and a cat in the bed with her, and was content.

The door of the room opened, and a small boy of about five came round it, hanging on to the edge.

'I'm busy,' Carol said.

'She s- she s-says, if if if you don't come dow- dow- down right away, she'll c-come up and and and hit you with the –' It was too awful to say. The child's eyes were blue and white saucers. His rosy mouth was pursed in alarm. 'With the –'

'Belt or broom handle? Ha ha, funny joke. I'm taller than her. I got too big for the belt years ago. You're not, though!' Laughing, she made a lunge off the bed at the chubby little boy, and chased him down the stairs roaring, the child shrieking, half with fear, half with glee.

Was this the child whom she had heard crying? Rose wondered, as she clattered down the bare stairs with Carol. No, too old. That had been a baby's cry.

'Knock it off, you two.' The woman at the sink, pounding with massive red arms at the clothes in the suds, was as broad as she was high. Her scarlet face, shining on the cheeks and the little round upturned tip of her nose, was framed by brown hair cut like a child's and caught up at one side with a Mickey Mouse slide. She coughed through a cigarette stuck on her lower lip.

'Change little Davey, there's a love.'

In spite of the threats and the husky voice that coughed in the smoke and steam, she was really quite easy going.

'Change little Davey, there's a love.' She grinned gummily at Carol. She had taken her teeth out to do the washing. They were in a soup bowl on the dresser that filled one wall of the cramped and cluttered kitchen.

Below her, a boy of about two with a running nose and cough was staggering about with a torn jersey on the top of him and nothing on the bottom except a sagging nappy which all too obviously needed changing.

Was he the crying child? Was that why the horse had brought her here?

While Carol and Rose changed him on the floor, with gentle words of love, and chuckles from the happy baby, a boy and girl of about fourteen and fifteen came in from school.

Where did everybody sleep in this apparently small house? From the assortment of clothes and toys in Carol's bedroom and the state of the bed, it looked as if she and little Davey and stammering Gregory were in there together.

The older brother and sister were continuing a fight they had brought in from the street. Carol turned up the radio to drown them out. Gregory fell over the cat, which had a fish head on the floor, and it shrieked. Davey shrieked and clutched his mother round her stout legs, and she shrieked too, and swatted at him. It was a raucous, slap-happy family, quick to yell and hit out, but just as quick to laughter.

Before the mother rinsed the clothes, she took two fistfuls of suds and smeared them round her cheeks and chin, and with the wet cigarette hanging out, she took a chopping knife and pretended to shave herself, for the amusement of Davey and Gregory.

'Dadda! Dadda!' Davey cried, and climbed on to the back of the lopsided sofa to look out of the window.

'Not yet, duckie. He's working an extra shift today

thank God.' But everyone agreed that David Morgan was the cleverest two-year-old ever.

'Make something of himself, he will, one of these days,' Mrs Morgan said, lifting up her apron to wipe the suds off her face. 'Unlike the rest of you juvenile delinquents.'

'Don't *say* that.' Her oldest son Arthur slapped her on her mountainous behind, which wore trousers as wide as the ones they get two clowns into at the circus. 'It's a delicate subject.'

Because Rose was inside Carol's mind, she knew that Arthur was due to go to court for some small pilfering jobs. No one in the family thought badly of him for that. They weren't in favour of pilfering; they were simply too loyal to believe he'd done it.

'It'll be a delicate subject for the police if I could get up in court and say what I thought of them.' The mother mauled and pummelled laundry in the grey scummy rinse water as if it were Constable Hanratty. He had it in for them, because they continued to live in a condemned dwelling the bulldozers were panting to demolish, since the Council had not been able to find housing for the large family, and because they were poor but honest, unlike some people in this town, who were rich and dishonest.

Which town? Rose had, of course, guessed by now that she might be in the house at the end of the dilapidated street, but was no wiser about where it was. When the wash was wrung out, she kept hoping that Carol would offer to take it out to the line in the back yard, so that Rose could get a good look round, but the mother dumped the basket on the older daughter, Mavis, who was making up her eyes at a tiny mirror tacked to the back of the door among the coats and scarves.

'If you fancy you're going out tonight with your fast friends,' she told her, 'think again. You've got three days homework to catch up with.'

'It's all done.'

'Liar.' Arthur knocked the eyeshadow brush out of her hand, and she bit his arm.

33

'She'll come to no good,' the mother sighed. She lit the gas under a pan full of fat on the encrusted stove, with a roar and a small explosion. 'Book learning is the only way to get yourself out of this hole. Look at me. I never had none, and I'm stuck. Stuck with you, my little darling angel boy.' She threw a fistful of potatoes into the fat, and turned away from the backfire of spitting steam to pick up little Davey and hoist him high up into the air until he could put the palms of his grubby paws on to the low ceiling, to join the other many paw marks.

Rose could not imagine her ever being cruel to this child, or leaving him alone. But when he slipped in her arms on the way down and nearly fell, he began to cry in fright, the same hoarse, wailing cry that Rose had been hearing off and on at the back of her mind ever since she was Linda with the awkward ankle strap. Or did all frightened babies with colds sound the same?

Stuck, Carol was thinking. She's stuck, like I'm not going to be. She went out of the kitchen and into the front room across the passage, where a bed with cushions against the wall doubled as a sofa, and knelt by the window sill with her elbows among the starving plants, and stared out past the edge of a torn blanket that was the curtain at the house across the street.

It was the same street. The house opposite was the one where the cat had been huddled in the window box. Rose could see the brick railway wall with the dark opening of the tunnel like Mrs Morgan's mouth without her teeth.

But Carol dreamed of white palaces and thirty storey hotels on the edge of a clear blue ocean, and herself in gorgeous glittering clothes stepping down a wide curved staircase to where a group of beautiful people raised champagne glasses and applauded her, because she was a star.

She got up and spread out her arms in the crumpled school blouse with frayed cuffs, and took a few waltzing turns in the small room. She pointed her toes and bent her

34

neck with a radiant smile to the blank screen of the television set, as if it were an audience.

Rose, who danced as if she were playing hockey, according to her father, liked the feeling of lightness, and the dizzying intoxication of whirling round and round with her arms out. The room spun round her. The bed, the broken gas fire, the television, the dry plants whizzed by and spun her like a flung pebble into a room full of noise, where she swayed and grabbed for the handle of the upright vacuum cleaner, which was roaring away as she had left it.

She stared out of the window to where the horse had been, and Mrs Ardis came in with her ritzy voice to ask her, 'Pray, why are you standing there with your mouth open? It's not the fly-catching season any more, as far as I've been informed.'

CHAPTER FIVE

When the Kellys arrived, late on Friday afternoon, Rose
was on the verandah collecting teacups and talking to
Elisabeth Engel, who had become less shy as the good air
of the ocean and the good friendly atmosphere of Wood
Briar did their work. Rose made a quick excuse and left
the tray and ducked into the hotel out of sight, as she
usually did when Ben arrived.

Why didn't she hurry out to greet him, as she would
have done if he were Abigail, or Jake and Julie, or Leonora
and Martin, or any of her good friends?

Because he was Ben, and each time he had been away,
she wondered if he would be changed, or more grown up,
or look different in some way.

He looked just the same as when he had left in August,
except that he was wearing a blue sweater instead of a blue
shirt, and had lost some of his tan. His nut-brown curly
hair was still short, to streamline him for running. He still
laughed tolerantly at his garrulous mother when she
started to carry on about the suitcases, and winked at his
father.

Rose, who had scuttled upstairs, observed him contentedly through a white lozenge of the round stained glass
window over the front door, then walked fairly slowly down
the stairs as the Kellys came into the hall.

'Rose!' Ben put down two bags and came to the bottom of
the stairs. 'Wow, it's good to be back. How's everything?'

'All right.' Rose stopped four steps above him.

'Well Rose goodness gracious you look wonderful you've
grown don't say you haven't because I can see you have
what do you think Jack?' Ben's mother's conversation ran
on like water flowing from a tap.

'If you say so, Marguerite.' Her tall, amiable husband flapped his hand to indicate, 'There she goes again.'

'I hope you're putting us in the annexe Rose dear you know how we love it and I've brought my own coffeepot this time because yours doesn't quite get the flavour we're accustomed to at home no offence but you know at Wood Briar we always feel so at home that's why we come here Mollie my dear how *are* you a sight for sore eyes!'

Rose's mother came down the back stairs from their own rooms with a smile of welcome.

'Back again. Can you stand it?' Mr Kelly said.

'Your family is one of the things that make it fun to run a hotel.' Mollie hugged him. She was a great one for loving embraces. Rose's father rebuked her for doing it to guests, however familiar. He said it was unprofessional.

Next morning, Rose went out early with Ben, as she always did, to pace him on his training run along the beach. She was out of condition.

'Why are you puffing?' Ben asked sternly, breathing easily as his feet marked the sand, one two, one two, smoothly and evenly.

'Well . . . I haven't been running every day, like you said.'

'Why not?'

'Too busy.' She couldn't say, 'It's no fun without you.'

'Want to run on the moor later – jump some ditches?' he asked, as she stopped at the breakwater.

'I can't. There's something I've got to do.'

'See you!' He jumped the breakwater and ran on, Jake and Julie's brown dog galloping behind him, and the seagulls rising before them in a clamour of wings and settling down again behind them to go on with their low tide scavenging.

What Rose had to do was to go into Newcome to try to discover if this was the town where the Morgans lived, and to try to find their street. To save time, she took the bus into town, got off at the railway station and started to walk down some of the streets near the line in the hope of finding the high embankment wall and the tunnel.

But these streets were not tumbledown. The houses and shops were small, and it was not a fancy neighbourhood, but the rows of terrace houses were all in fairly good repair, and occupied.

An old man was digging in a garden at the side of his house. Rose stopped by the fence and admired his michaelmas daisies, which rioted in every shade of pink and mauve and blue and purple. When he stopped digging, and rested a foot on his spade to talk to her, she asked him, in the sham casual style she had learned since she had started her secret life as the grey horse's messenger, 'Know any really grotty, sort of deserted streets round here?'

'Can't say I do. Why?'

'Well, I've got a friend, someone I know at school, and I was trying to find her. She told me she lived in a house that was supposed to be condemned.'

'If the house was condemned,' the old man said, lowering his whiskery white eyebrows at Rose, 'she'd not be living in it, no. The Council would never allow that, no.'

'But if they couldn't find a better house . . .'

'There's places enough for those that pay their way. There's too many people today who think the world owes them a living, and want to live free off the rest of us decent citizens who've always worked hard and paid our taxes.'

He had started off on what was evidently a favourite subject, so Rose said goodbye and disappeared.

'Excuse me.' A policeman stood in the doorway of a shop she passed, as she was exploring in a rough square that would bring her back to the station in time for the bus home. 'I'm looking for a friend who lives in a – in a sort of abandoned kind of street. Are there any places like that round here?'

'Search me,' the policeman said. 'I'm new here. Just moved down from the city.'

'It's near a high railway wall.' He looked at her as if she were talking an unknown language. 'With a tunnel under the line?'

He shook his head. The lack of an embankment wall was obvious to her anyway. From what she could see, the railway lines ran through a cutting at the end of some of the short neat streets she had looked at.

'Well, thanks.'

'Are you lost?' He saw disappointment in her face, and stepped forward, more interested.

'Me? Oh no.' She didn't want him to question her. 'I'm going to the bus.'

The door of the record shop opened on a burst of rock music as two customers came out. When the door closed and shut off the music, another sound drifted through Rose's head, the haunting sound of the crying child. She walked quickly away down the hill to the station.

Gloria, one of the extra maids who came in the summer and at weekends, had brought her two-year-old grandson today, because her daughter was working. He sat at the kitchen table, fingering grubby balls of dough while Gloria rolled pastry for the fruit pies. He was the same age as little Davey Morgan, and he too had a runny nose and a cough that sounded like a bagful of rusty nails, as only a toddler's cough can.

Obsessed with following the clues of the crying child and the Morgan family, and terribly anxious about Davey, Rose decided to conduct an experiment to try to reassure herself that all toddlers with colds cried the same way, and that Davey's crying didn't mean danger.

'Can I take Barry outside?' she asked Gloria.

'Help yourself. Heaven knows he needs the air, with that wicked chest of his. My daughter keeps him cooped up indoors too much, if you ask me.'

'Come on then.' Rose lifted Barry down and he followed her trustingly, not knowing what he was in for. She took him out to the back lawn, where Ben was practising his putting shots on the clock golf circle.

'Ben.' She interrupted his concentration on an easy shot into the hole from the four o'clock marker. 'I need to try something.'

'What?' He missed the hole, and looked up.

'Well –' the sham casual voice again – 'we're doing this play at school, you see, and I'm sort of the noises off – you know – coconuts for horse's hoofs, ringing the church bells, going "rhubarb, rhubarb", to sound like an angry crowd at the gates, making the noise of a baby crying.'

'Sounds like a star part.'

'It's fun, but I'm not quite sure about the baby. It's supposed to be about Barry's age, and it's frightened.' She did not look at him when she was inventing. 'The mother – that's my friend Hazel in a long black skirt of Miss Hennessy's – is just going to betray her country to the enemy, but she hears her baby crying because the police are breaking in, and she rushes out of the room, falling over the skirt, good old Hazel, and the police rush in and capture the spy.'

Ben half closed his eyes and looked at her tolerantly, as he did when his mother was babbling.

'So you can see, the baby's very important. I've got to get it right. Gloria's got the radio turned up, so let's frighten poor Barry and see what he sounds like.'

'Poor little kid.'

'He won't mind. Gloria says he cries half the time anyway, just for the exercise of it, and I've got some sweets in my pocket. I'll get his attention, and you come up behind and go "Boo".'

'It was your idea,' Ben said. 'You do it.'

He knocked the ball neatly into the hole, and Barry plunged forward on to his knees to pick it out.

'Boo!' Rose cried behind him, and instantly wished she hadn't. He sat down with his legs stuck out and the golf ball in his hands and bawled in shrill, sharp yelps. Normal two-year-old rage. Nothing at all like Davey Morgan's hoarse terror. Rose picked him up and hugged him and gave him a sweet. He recovered immediately, and she didn't think she had damaged him for life, but she felt guilty. That couldn't be the way messengers were supposed to do the horse's noble work.

And sure enough, as she put the child down and he trotted after Ben towards the marker for five o'clock, a rush and a roar and the thunder of galloping hoofs overwhelmed Rose, and she fell flat on her face, while Favour's wrath swept over her.

She got up and said, 'I'm sorry,' into the air.

'I don't mind,' Ben said. 'But when you trip over the ten o'clock marker and pull it out of the ground, just put it back, there's a good girl.'

At least she knew. All two-year-old cries of fright were not the same. One experiment did not prove it exactly, and she wasn't going to do another, even if she knew another toddler, but she knew now that those had been cries of terror in the deserted street, and that Davey was in danger.

Why? When? In the past or in the future, or now this very minute? What did the horse want her to do about it?

She wanted to discuss it with Mr Vingo, but he was out on the beach with Elisabeth Engel, looking for shells. He was trying to help her to get her nerves back into shape after her breakdown, and she was trying to help him to get his figure back into shape, although he said it was a lost cause, since he had been this shape ever since he could remember.

CHAPTER SIX

Rose was clearing dinner tables with her mother, when Ben came back into the dining-room with that look in his eyes that meant he had a scheme going.

'There's a full moon,' he said. 'Jake and Julie and I are going up to the old castle ruins to look for ghosts. Want to come?'

'Oh *yes*,' Rose said at once. She would have said yes to anything he suggested, because she had been afraid he was annoyed with her about making the baby cry. But then she looked at the state of the dining-room and had to say, 'No, I can't,' because there was a lot of work still to do.

'Can't what?' Her mother came by with a tray full of salt and pepper shakers to be filled.

'I'm trying to get her to go ghost hunting,' Ben said. 'Jake and Julie want to go, but Rose doesn't dare.'

'Of course she dares. You go, Rose. Gloria and I can finish up here. Have fun. See ghosts. You've done enough work for one day.'

Mr Vingo was finishing a late dinner at his corner table. He had come down late, because he had been playing the piano and forgotten the time.

When Rose and Ben said goodnight to him, he asked Ben through a mouthful of Gloria's blackberry pie, 'Do you really think the ruins above the lake are haunted?'

'No, of course not. I don't believe in that stuff. It's just a joke really. We want to play at spooks.'

Ben was laughing, but Mr Vingo, leaning forward over his plate, with blackberry juice on his chin and his eyes turned up to them with the whites showing, looked serious. He swallowed, coughed and said, 'Be careful.'

'Oh, we will,' Ben said.

Rose said nothing, although the warning was directed at her.

Jake and Julie were a bright and lively young couple, who both worked in offices in the city fifty miles away and used their Wood Briar weekends, they said, to preserve their sanity.

In the city, they were quite important people who wore business clothes and carried briefcases and went to meetings where large sums of money were discussed, but at Wood Briar they wore terrible old clothes and were like children playing, always looking for new ideas for amusement.

'Mrs Ardis says the man who once lived in the castle was the devil incarnate,' Julie said in the car, with the brown dog on her lap and her arms round its neck. 'She says no one should go up there at night, and she doesn't expect to see us in bed when she brings in the early morning tea tomorrow.'

'Don't worry,' Rose said. 'It's Sunday. She won't be on duty early. I'll bring in your tea.'

'She says –' Julie hugged the dog and shivered, to try to get herself into a spooky mood – 'that campers who pitch tents up there have been known to come down the hill in the morning with their eyes staring and their hair turned stark white.'

'What did they see?' Rose asked. She knew a lot about the castle ruins on the hill above the lake. Mr Vingo had told her the truth about the legend of the grey horse Favour who had been a charger of the Lord of the Moor, who lived there. She had even once glimpsed the spirit of the wicked Lord, as well as seeing and hearing his soldiers, in the swirling mists of the secret valley.

'It was too dreadful to tell,' Julie said, deep and solemn, like Mrs Ardis when she was using her doom voice, and burst into laughter.

The moon was high, and its light lay on the hill like snow as they left the car and climbed up to the few remaining piles of stones and the solitary jagged wall that was all that was left of the old lookout tower.

At the top, they sat on the stones and drank in the beauty of the night. Before them, the moor stretched away to the dark masses of the distant hills. Above them, the dark side of the tower wall reached like a finger across the moon, next to it, the broken arch of what had once been a gateway. Below them, a sheet of silver was the lake.

'Why do they call it Noah's Bowl?' Jake asked.

'Because it was a valley before the flooded river filled it,' Rose said.

'This is all much too calm and beautiful. It isn't spooky at all.'

To put that right, Jake slipped off the stone wall and disappeared behind some bushes that grew round the base of the tower, so they could wonder where he was and when he was going to pounce on them.

After some hiding and dodging and chasing each other among the black shadows in the intoxicating moonlight, Julie disappeared too. While Jake was still making ghostly wails from behind the tower wall and his dog was howling, either at him or at the moon, a shrouded figure suddenly appeared under the archway.

Rose's heart leaped up into her throat, and she felt the roots of her hair stiffen. But the dog's howls changed to barking and he leaped joyously at the figure and tore off the sheet that Julie had run back to get from the boot of the car.

'Sorry, Rose.' Julie shook out her hair and started to wrap herself in the sheet, while the dog still hung on to the end of it. 'I didn't mean to scare you.' She wound the sheet tightly round herself. 'Secrets of the mummy's tomb,' she intoned. 'Where is the foul grave robber, Benjamin, who has been foolhardy enough to open my sepulchre and unloose the curse of a thousand ages?'

'Over there. I heard him shouting.'

'You didn't.' Ben suddenly dropped to the ground from the jagged top of the tower.

'Jake!' Rose called. She could still hear the muffled shouts. But Jake continued to wail away among the bushes.

44

A shrouded figure suddenly appeared . . .

The shouts came nearer, and there was a clatter of hoofs on stone, and a rush of movement as a white blur sped past Rose through the remains of the arch, kicking up a pebble against her leg. Below her where the valley used to be, she heard a roaring, clamorous sound like a torrent of water. She heard dogs barking in frenzy, the bleating of lambs.

'What's up, Rosie?'

She had fallen to her knees on the turf, staring down the hill towards the shining waters of the lake. Beside her, the brown dog was whining, his legs stiff, the hair on his back raised.

Rose looked back at Ben over her shoulder. 'Didn't you see?'

'See what?'

'Didn't you see him rush by?'

'See who? Come on, you've got to do better than that, for a ghost.'

'But the wind, and the dogs . . . Couldn't you hear the water?'

'No takers,' Ben said, and Julie said comfortably, 'She's possessed, poor soul. Come on, Rose, it's time to go home. There aren't any ghosts here and the game's over.'

Jake whistled to the dog. 'Stop looking for rabbits.' He put a hand on the dog, who came out of his trance and cringed, yawning and licking his hand, his eyes confused.

As Rose got up, she felt a sharp pain on her shin. Putting down a hand, she felt a trickle of blood oozing from a small cut where the pebble flung up by the hoofs had hit her.

'I wish,' Rose said to Mr Vingo's broad back, 'you'd stop playing and listen to me.'

He lifted his right hand from the treble end of the piano and waved at her. She had to wait until he had finished the 'March of the Dead Men's Souls', and played the last reverberating chord, which rattled the windows and made Rose fear for the stability of the sloping floor. One day, Mr Vingo and his marmalade piano were going to find themselves through the floor and down on to the side verandah, probably still playing.

He swung round on the stool, and he and Rose both said together, 'I've got something to tell you.'

She wanted to tell him about the clues and what she had seen and heard at the castle ruins, but he was full of his own news, so she had to let him tell it first.

'Listen, Rose of all Roses.' His dark protuberant eyes glistened. 'Your friend R. V. Vingo is going to be famous at last.'

'What for?'

'I've been talking to people at the music department of the University, getting some ideas from them to help me with the orchestration of the Ballad. And you know what?' The intense, dramatic chords of the march had shortened his breath. He panted for a moment before he went on. 'They've asked me to give a performance of the first part of the Ballad of Favour at the University, in front of an audience.'

'How wonderful.'

'A small audience, you understand. My nerves couldn't stand playing before a large concert hall group. But they *want* me, Rose, just think of it.'

He was amazingly modest for such a knowledgeable and talented man. Somehow Rose felt as if she were older than him, and had to say, 'I'm proud of you,' as if she were his mother. 'Now I've got something –'

Before she could tell him her news, feet clattered on the winding stair that corkscrewed up to the turret room, and Abigail knocked on the door. She came in wearing a thick cable-knit sweater and jodhpurs and boots, her lively face flushed with colour from the chilly day.

'Where you been?' Rose asked, although she had seen her at school this morning.

'Riding over. Crackers is tied to the drainpipe behind the toolshed.'

Rose looked at her watch. 'O.K. Dad won't be home for a bit.'

'Mr Vingo and I are going to practise our duet.' Abigail had her flute in its case in a satchel on her back. 'We're getting better at it. When we're ready, we're going to perform for you.'

'We're going to do better than that,' Mr Vingo said. 'We're going to perform it in front of a small but select audience.'

'At the concert?' Rose asked in delight.

'Why not? The "Dancing Song of the Valley People" belongs in the first part of the Ballad.' He told Abigail about the plans for the concert.

'Hey, I'm not good enough yet,' she said, but Rose could see that she was longing to give it a try.

'Then we shall practise some more.' Mr Vingo swung back to the piano and shuffled the music about on the stand, then flexed his fingers while Abigail took out her flute and poised it to her lips. Then he beat his foot and counted, 'One, two, three –' and they plunged together into the gay music.

Mr Vingo swayed slightly to the rhythm of the dancing beat. Abigail looked charming in her riding clothes with her hair in a thick pigtail down her back, and her whole face concentrated into the flute. Listening entranced, Rose forgot her impatience at not being able to tell Mr Vingo what had been happening to her, and was filled with happiness, because she had two friends like these.

CHAPTER SEVEN

On the night of the concert, Abigail looked even more charming. Her thick chestnut hair was loose round her shoulders, rippling with deep waves where it had been plaited. She wore a sort of peasant dress with a wide low neck and full sleeves.

She and Rose sat near the front of the small hall, so that she could go up to the piano at the right time. Everyone was there. There were about twenty people from the University. Abigail and her parents, Rose and her parents. Sam, Mollie's catering friend from Newcome Hollow, who had brought refreshments. From Wood Briar, Elisabeth Engel; two German women who were doing a tour of English cathedrals; a doctor and his wife who were waiting to move into a flat near the hospital; a travelling salesman who always played Draughts with Mr Vingo when he stayed at the hotel.

There were no programmes, but Elisabeth Engel was to speak the introduction. Mr Vingo had written it for her, and encouraged her to do this for him, as part of the building up of her self-confidence, which was what she needed after her illness.

As she stepped on to the low stage, the audience grew quiet. She wore a pale dress with a blue pendant, and her ash blonde hair was brushed out long and loose behind her ears and behind her shoulders.

This was the night for loose hair, it seemed. Rose had washed hers and rinsed it twice, once in beer and once in lemon juice, to make it light and fluffy, but when she saw Elisabeth, she whispered to Abigail, 'Shall I grow my hair?'

'Forget it,' Abigail whispered back out of the side of her mouth.

Behind Rose, Philip Wood sighed and muttered, 'I hope she's not going to recite poetry.'

Rose pretended not to know him.

Holding the papers, but not looking at them, Elisabeth looked at the audience, blinked her pale lashes several times and started to speak. Only Rose and Abigail saw that her hands were trembling, and that underneath the skirt of her light dress her legs were trembling.

'You've come to hear the music,' she started. 'Not to hear me talk.'

Philip Wood grunted something that might have been, 'Hear, hear,' and Mollie poked him with her elbow.

'But so that you can understand the music better, we want you to know something of the legend that lies behind *The Ballad of the Great Grey Horse*.' Elisabeth put up a finger to hook her hair back behind her ear. 'It's a true story.' Philip Wood snorted gently. 'You may have heard different versions of it if you've lived round here for some time, but the truth of it is like this.' She hooked her hair back again.

'Once there was rich and evil man who called himself the Lord of the Moor, although he was nobody's Lord by right of birth or royal decree. He lived in a grim castle on the moor where the ruins on the hill are now, and grabbed for himself the grazing and forests that used to be common land for the farmers and peasants who lived in the valley below the castle. He grabbed their best cattle and horses too, and their prettiest daughters to be servants, and wives for the brutal band of soldiers in his private army.'

Elisabeth had stopped trembling. Telling the story in her clear and gentle voice, she had caught the attention of the audience. Abigail was leaning forward, absorbed, her elbows on her knees and her head in her hands.

'One of the horses at the castle was a magnificent grey horse of great speed and courage.' Rose smiled to herself. 'He was called Favour, because he was the favourite charger of the wicked Lord of the Moor. One of the children at the

50

castle was the son of a soldier and a girl from the valley. He was called Alan, and he was just about thirteen. Because the Lord had cut down the trees on the river bank for gain, the river burst its banks after heavy storms and flooded the whole valley. The people who lived there were saved by Alan and Favour, galloping ahead of the rushing water to warn them.' Elisabeth stopped, and hooked her hair behind her ear again, although it had not escaped.

'I don't believe a word of it,' Rose's father muttered.

'It's *true*!' Rose turned and whispered to him fiercely.

'*The Ballad of the Great Grey Horse* is a song of praise for this noble deed.'

Elisabeth turned to Mr Vingo, who had been sitting at the side of the hall, listening to her intently, as if he had never heard the legend before. Now he stood up, wearing a black velvet jacket which Mollie had steamed and pressed, and a black bow tie hiding the fact that his shirt collar was too tight and wouldn't button, and lumbered shyly to the piano, wringing his hands to loosen them.

The first part of the music was beautiful. You could tell that the audience loved it, and Mr Vingo played better than Rose had ever heard him.

Then he paused, and announced, 'For the "Dancing Song of the Valley People", I will be joined by my colleague, Miss Abigail Drew.'

'Here goes nothing,' Abigail whispered to Rose. She stood up and stepped on to the platform. When she turned round, Rose saw that she was blushing, right up to the edges of her hair. She had never seen Abigail blush before.

Mr and Mrs Drew clapped, so everybody clapped, and Rose's father looked enthusiastic for the first time. Mr Vingo raised his hands above the keyboard. Abigail raised the flute to her lips with her fingers poised, and they were off.

Rose was so proud of them. These are my friends, she wanted people to know. Even though she was no dancer, the joyful music made her want to get up and dance, and she

51

noticed that many people were tapping their feet and smiling, and wagging their heads a bit.

Applause. Mr Vingo and Abigail took a bow, holding hands. Then Abigail hurried back to her seat and said, 'Phew!' and leaned back and stuck her legs out and flapped a hand to fan herself.

With that anxiety over, Rose could give herself up to the music. Some of it she knew. Some was new to her. Some of it was overwhelming, a tumbling waterfall of sound, and great melodic chords that reached into her soul. She closed her eyes and let the music capture her and carry her away into a kind of waking dream.

When she opened her eyes, she was not in the concert hall. The music was still running through her head, but she was out of doors. It was not like a scene from any of the journeys she had made with Favour. She did not seem to be anyone, or to have a body or a personality. No one was aware of her, but she could see and hear, as an observer, as if she were watching a film.

She saw the castle on the hill above the valley as it had been centuries ago at the time of the legend, a grim stone fortress with narrow windows, dominating the landscape. The square tower stood beside the arched stone gateway. The gate was of thick studded timber. Outside it on the grass, trodden and muddied by many hoofs, a poorly clad man was standing under the grey and lowering sky, with his cap in his hand, small and scared and overwhelmed by the menace of the castle.

Then, as if she could pass through those thick walls, Rose was in the great courtyard inside the castle walls. She saw the men, the same hateful soldiers she had glimpsed among the mists of the valley. She heard their laughter and their rough voices, heard the stamp of their boots on the stones, smelled the smoke of their fires, heard and smelled the horses, and saw them tethered in a long open shed at one side of the courtyard.

One of them was Favour. She would know him anywhere. He was not glowing and unearthly and larger than life, as he was when he appeared to her on the rock above the bridge. He had somehow taken earthly life and substance as a real horse like the others, but much finer and more restive and proud. He pulled back from his tether, and when one of the men cursed him and lifted an arm at him, he danced sideways and arched his neck with his ears back. The man hit him with a stick, and Favour squealed and stamped his hoof as if the man were under it.

'Don't hit him, Father.' A young boy, coming to the shed with a forkful of hay as big as himself, dropped his load, and went to the horse to put his hand on his neck and calm him. 'That's not the way to handle Favour.'

'Damn you, Alan.' The man hit out at his son, and the horse grabbed for him with his teeth.

'Bite me, would you?' He raised the stick again, but another soldier called out, 'Leave him be. The Lord is coming.'

A door in the castle opened. The sentries beside it straightened up and rang their pikes down on the stones. Out of the door stepped a small crooked man with a limp. The pale mouth in his white face was set in a sneer. His thin hair was like oiled wire. He wore a black tunic with a fur collar and a heavy gold chain. On his shoulder crouched a tiny brown weasel, its teeth murderous, its lips drawn back in an expression as loathsome as its master's.

This was the Lord of the Moor, the same horrible figure that Rose had seen in the valley mists and had hoped never to have to see again.

'So. Bring the fellow to me,' the Lord commanded in his thin cold voice with the nasty hissing lisp. 'If he's had the courage to come here, he may as well get his moneysworth.'

A small door within the great studded door was opened, and the man from outside stepped through, touching his forelock to the Lord and stopping several yards away from him.

'What is it now, Farmer Jarvis?' the Lord asked impatiently. 'Why do you people always bother me?'

The farmer straightened up and put back his shoulders and stuck out his chin and put a foot forward with the knee bent, to show he was not intimidated.

'I've come to speak for us all,' he said. 'I come in protest. Things are going badly for us in the valley, and we can't afford the taxes you impose on us.'

'If thingth are going badly,' the Lord lisped, 'it's your own fault, becauth you are lathy workers and hopeleth farmerth.'

'That is not true. You know it.' The man looked as if he was going to step forward, and the sentries shook their pikes and growled at him. 'But we haven't a chance with you taking away our common grazing and demanding your share of all we grow.'

'What a shame.' The Lord half closed his eyes and yawned, and the weasel yawned too, showing its killer fangs and a thin darting tongue like a snake. 'Thank you for coming to tell me.' He looked at the sky. 'Devils in hell,' he muttered. 'It's raining again. Is there no peath?'

'And that's another thing.' Two of the soldiers had moved towards the man to take him out, but he held his ground. 'The river is rising. Since you've cut down so much of our oak forest to sell for ships' timbers, the banks of the river are weakened.'

'Oh,' said the Lord, mocking the farmer's angry face through his slitted eyes. 'Thatth very alarming.'

'You can laugh.' The farmer clenched his fists. 'But one day there'll be a disaster.'

The Lord did laugh, a whining rattle high in his nose. He shook the rain from his oily curls and limped inside. The soldiers laughed and jeered coarsely at the farmer, and he allowed himself to be jostled through the small door in the big door.

Outside in the rain, which was now deluging down like steel rods, the man shook his fist at the castle door. Then he untied a thin old horse that was trying to shelter under a dead tree, and rode away, slumped and defeated, down the hill.

All along, Rose had been aware of the sound of Mr Vingo's piano behind what she saw and heard, like film music. It flowed through her head like a torrent, and she found herself down in the valley, where the rain was falling out of the sky in solid sheets of water.

The boy Alan was driving a few sheep into a hollow space behind a jutting flat rock. Drenched, he stood out on the rock to watch the river, and Rose saw that it was the same rock where the horse appeared to her, and the bridge below, with the river surging over the foot planks, was the same bridge she had to cross between her old familiar world and the new dream world with Favour.

Alan looked down the valley towards the sea, where the houses and farms and fishing village were hidden by the rain, and then back to the swollen river, shouldering its way against the embankments. Just above the bridge, he saw to his horror that the bank of earth and rocks was crumbling. Water was beginning to leak through over the valley floor.

Leaving his sheep, he clambered back up to the castle. Rose was with him, the music hurrying, hurrying. She saw him try to rouse the soldiers in the guardroom.

'The embankment is breached! Come out and help! Drag stones and timber – do something – the people are in danger!'

But the soldiers were drinking, and only laughed at him.

With a sob of rage, Alan ran through the courtyard where the horses stood in the shed, their tails tucked in against the driving rain. The main door was barred, but Alan knew all the secret ways of the castle. He squeezed through a narrow opening between two huge stones with grinning faces carved into them, their beaked noses dripping rain. He ran up a steep spiral stair inside a turret, then out into the lashing storm along an open battlement, fighting the wind to get to the far turret. Its door was locked, but he was small enough to crawl through an observation slit, grazing his elbows and knees. He hurtled down another spiral stair, falling the last few steps, then picked himself up and ran down a dark damp corridor and through the chill of a storage chamber that smelled of rotten meat. Dead animals and birds on hooks swung against him as he pushed through. In the doorway, he ducked past a group of servants carrying sacks. They shouted at him, and he shouted back and followed the twisting stone passages, dimly lit with barred windows, to the very centre of this evil place. The chamber of the Lord of the Moor himself.

The music pounded urgently in Rose's head as she saw Alan, panting and desperate, burst into the vaulted room. The light was dim. Flaring candles showed the rich hangings and weapons and horns and helmets that hung on the walls. An oil lamp hung from a beam on an iron chain fashioned like a snake, with its head upturned above the lamp and its fangs out to strike. In the pool of yellow light, the Lord sat in an enormous carved chair on a raised platform. The back was higher than his head and the seat could have accommodated three of him between the dragons which were its arms.

He sat like a child, with his feet dangling in their small pointed boots, stroking the slithery weasel on his lap as if it were a pet kitten.

In spite of his desperation, Alan remembered to drop on one knee in front of him.

'The embankment has been breached!' he gasped. 'Save the people!'

'Oh, well.' The Lord put his greasy head on one side, and his bony white claw continued to stroke the back of the mean little animal, which bared its teeth at Alan with a hiss. 'Perhaps we should just let them go. At least there will be no more trouble.'

'You can't, my Lord. A flood is coming. You've got to make the men fortify the embankments. You've got to do something.'

The horse sprang forward . . .

'Oh, but we can't thtop the fortheth of nature,' the Lord lisped smugly. 'If a flood is their fate, they mutht accthept it.'

'Send warning to them. They'd have time to escape.'

'Too late.' The Lord lifted his lip in a sneering, crooked smile. 'No one could get there in time.'

'Favour could.' Alan stood boldly upright. He knew what he had to do.

The Lord scowled. 'No one rides Favour but me.'

'Today *I* do!'

As the Lord struggled down from the high throne, Alan escaped from the chamber, through the labyrinth of corridors and twisting steps and out to the courtyard. He dragged open one side of the heavy gate, then darted back to untie the rope of the grey horse's halter.

Favour backed out at once into the teeming rain, and Alan leaped on to his back, just as the Lord came running out of the castle with a sword in his hand to stop him. Scuttling on the wet flagstones, he was before Alan at the gate, his arm raised to slash down with the sword, but the horse sprang forward and trampled him on to the stones like a bundle of black rags, the red blood washing away into the gurgling gutters.

As Alan and Favour galloped out under the arch, and headlong down the hill to the river bank, Rose saw a tiny travelling ribbon of movement as the weasel slithered away through the wet grass.

The music swelled and drowned out everything else with the roar of a torrent of water. A hand fell on Rose's shoulder, and her father's voice said in her ear, 'You can wake up now, Rose. It's over.'

The music had stopped. The roar of water had dwindled into the sound of clapping hands. Mr Vingo was standing up and bowing, breathing heavily and sweating, leaning on the piano as if he would fall down without it. Rose looked round at her parents. Mollie nodded, beaming and applauding hard, nudging Philip to make him clap harder.

'Did you like it?' Rose asked.

'I'd like to go through it all again.' Her mother's eyes were dreamy, as if she too, like Rose, had been in another world.

'It wasn't as bad as I expected,' her father said. 'Bit noisy.'

'We thought it was fantastic,' Abigail said, 'didn't we, Rose?'

'She slept through most of it,' Rose's father said.

'Well, so would you if you worked as hard as she did – oops, sorry, Mr Wood, nothing against you – but people like Rose who are short on sleep do drop off when they sit down.'

Had she been asleep? Was it all a dream? It was much too vivid for that. Rose's heart was still racing with the urgency and drama of what she had witnessed. She could still see, as clearly as if it were there on the varnished wood floor in front of her, the wet black trampled body of the Lord of the Moor, with the blood flowing swiftly away with the rain.

During the refreshments, several people came up to Mr Vingo to congratulate him and tell him to be sure and come back to play the rest of the Ballad, when it was finished. He smiled modestly, but he was too short of breath to talk much to them.

As people left, and Mollie and Sam were clearing up, Mr Vingo went to sit in a chair in the back row, to wait for the car.

Rose sat down beside him.

'I saw it all,' she said quickly.

He nodded. 'I thought you did.'

'What happens after Alan and Favour gallop out down the valley?'

'They race the flood waters, and in a tremendous leap – no. You'll have to wait till I've written it.'

'It is true, isn't it? You didn't make it up?'

'Rose!' He looked shocked.

'Save the people!' Rose said softly.

59

'He did. Still does. *You* know.'

'Yes, and I know what it is this time. A child in danger,' Rose whispered. 'I know who he is, but not where, or why. I don't know what to do.'

'You will, brave messenger, as Alan knew.'

'Was he one of us?'

Mr Vingo nodded. 'He answered the call. You too. Be ready.'

CHAPTER EIGHT

After the concert, Mr Vingo was not exactly famous, but he had made a dent. There were two paragraphs in the local newspaper calling him Mr Virgo. Someone rang up for piano lessons, which were not in his line. A friend of Philip Wood who had invented a new kind of tin opener wanted him to write a jingle for it that could be played at a forthcoming Kitchen Fair. A university professor's wife and her daughter, who had talked to Sam and Mollie at the concert, came to the hotel to make a last-minute request to have the daughter's wedding reception there, since there had been a fire in the restaurant where she was going to have it.

Their first wedding at Wood Briar. Mollie went into a fever of plans and arrangements. Mrs Ardis said the hotel was getting ideas beyond its station. Dilys said, 'A bride – some people get all the luck.' Gloria said, 'I'm going to clean this old place from top to bottom, you see if I'm not.' Abigail booked herself up to help Rose on the great day.

Meanwhile, the rest of life went back to normal. Mr Vingo disappeared again for a bit. Rose and Abigail went to the stables for a jumping lesson with Joyce.

Rose was afraid of jumping. Approaching every jump, she could not help imagining all the things that could go wrong.

It was lovely when it went right, and Moonlight lurched over without breaking the rhythm of his lumbering canter. That did not often happen, largely because Rose expected him to stop, or run out, or stumble when he landed and push his pink nose through the mud until he got his feet back, and so he usually did.

Why did she jump? Because Joyce said she had to.

Because one of her life's beliefs, stronger since she knew Favour, was that you had to make yourself do things you didn't want to do. Because Abigail said, 'C'mon, old Rose, it's much more fun if we do it together.'

Abigail was going to take her dun pony into some junior classes before the show season ended. Crackers was a skilled and eager jumper who could manage a clear round at small shows if he felt like it. But he had his off days, and so did Abigail. Sometimes he would rush the jumps and take off too close. Sometimes he would run out at the last moment. Sometimes Abigail's mind was on higher things and she forgot the course, even though she had watched fifteen people jump it before her.

She was pleased with a win or a place, but what she really liked was the jumping and the excitement, and showing off spunky little Crackers. She actually did not care much if she won or not, which was just as well, since the prizes were usually won by the gimlet-eyed children who rode to win and never forgot the course.

Joyce cared if Abigail won. It was a good advertisement for the stable, since she took lessons there. She had put up sizeable jumps in the middle of the field – 'Here goes nothing,' Abigail told Crackers as she circled him into a canter to start the first round – and smaller ones round the edge of the field for Rose and Moonlight and a tiny child called Lulu, who was learning to jump on a huge brown horse who was called Safety First, because he had been in the business a long time.

'All *right*!' Abigail and Crackers were having a good day. Joyce put the jumps up and the pony cleared them again neatly.

'Your reins were too long, your bottom sticks out, you judged him all wrong at the wall.' Joyce could always find something to criticize. She stood in the middle of the field with a long lungeing whip, not necessarily to use on the horses. She just liked to hold it.

'All right, you two landlubbers over there by the hedge.

et's see if you've learned anything from watching Abbie nd Crack.' She never bothered with anyone's full name. Rose was Ro. Moonlight was Mule. Lulu and the clever, areful brown horse were Lu and Safe.

Perched on his back like a midget jockey, Lulu, who was only eight, set her jaw, and the big horse carried her over he tree trunk and two rails and a double line of hay bales ike a champion. He jumped them once more, and then tarted back to the gate, since Lulu was not strong enough o stop him.

'All right, Lu!' Joyce strode across to grab his rein before he got to the gate. 'Naughty boy, stop playing games with ittle kids.' She slapped him chummily on the neck. If it had een Moonlight, she would have yanked at his rein and aid, 'Knock that off, you ugly mule. What the hell do you hink you're doing?'

Moonlight did not want to jump. Rose could sense that, ven as she trotted to the end of the field and turned him owards the fallen tree trunk. She could not even make him anter.

'Push! Push, girl, push!' Joyce yelled and came towards hem holding out the long whip, but Moonlight stopped at he fallen tree, then lurched over it from a standstill, leaving Rose off balance, so that she leaned backwards and jerked im in the mouth.

'All wrong.' Joyce shook her hair, which had been cut ery short and permed into a thousand curls. 'Get him oing, Ro. Come on, you lazy mule.' She flicked the whip ound his tail and he put his ears back.

'I don't think he wants to jump,' Rose said.

'He hasn't got the brains to think.'

'He feels funny.' Moonlight had landed stiffly. 'Perhaps omething's wrong?'

'There's nothing wrong with him that a good kick in the ibs won't cure. Come on, Ro, use your legs. Legs, I said!'

Somehow, Rose got him over one rail and the hay bales, ecause she was too scared not to. At the last rail, she said,

63

'I'm sorry, Moon,' as she kicked him. He took off half-heartedly, broke the rail as he crashed through it, and stumbled on the other side. Rose fell off.

'Get back on!' Joyce ordered, but Rose walked away across the field with the reins over her arm and the horse's head nodding low beside her. 'Get on!'

'You don't have to.' Abigail got off Crackers and led him beside Rose. 'Are you O.K.?' Rose nodded. 'That was bad luck.'

'No, it wasn't.'

'Hey, you *are* hurt. What happened?'

'Nothing I'm O.K.' Rose was crying silently, but not from physical pain.

'I'll give you a lesson on Crackers at home,' Abigail said. 'You could do real well. Don't let that female commando get you down.'

Rose shook her head. She was not crying for herself.

In the stable, she bent to run her hand over Moonlight's legs, not sure what she was looking for, but knowing that something was wrong. There did seem to be a slight swelling at the back of one bony knee.

'His left leg is swollen,' Rose told Joyce when she stuck her tight curls over the loosebox door to see why Rose had not brought the saddle and bridle to the tack room.

Joyce squinted down at the leg. 'Nothing to speak of. He's stiffening up a bit, that's all. Happens to all old horses.'

'Poor Moon.' Rose came back from the tack room and leaned over the door to watch the cream-coloured horse pulling at his hay greedily to fill the great hollows within him, and dropping some of it into the water bucket. Holding a mouthful of water, he stuck out his head to Rose and slobbered it over her hands, before he went back to his hay rack.

As she stood and watched him, he changed. His coat whitened and dappled and began to shine like a pearl. His head was smaller and finer and his neck more arched, his body filled out and muscular, his pale eye deep and gleaming. There was a misty glow about him, like a lamp shining through fog. He was Favour.

Then Rose's eyes re-focussed, and he was only poor old Moonlight, with a manure stain on his rump she had not been able to brush out, and a loose sheaf of hay trailing from his slack pink lips.

The message was clear. Even if the tune had not started to curl through her mind in a spiralling flight of melody, she would have known that the grey horse was calling her.

'Got to go,' she told Moonlight, the only one besides Mr Vingo for whom she did not have to invent an excuse.

Abigail had ridden home. Rose took her bicycle as far as she could on the bridle path that went up to the moor, then left it under a tree and ran towards the foot of the hill where the castle ruins stood above the lake. Noah's Bowl was gone, as she knew it would be.

The white mist hung thickly in the valley. Rose thought about the soldiers whose ghosts might be waiting there, the men she had seen in the flesh of a bygone time when she was carried away from the concert to watch the origin of the legend. In this mist, which was dense and still, not swirling and thinning and gathering again, it was impossible to watch for them.

Feeling her way cautiously down, she shrank with the dread that she would brush against a cloak, feel a reeking breath on her cheek without seeing a face, hear the same brutal laughter that had defeated the farmer and now waited to defeat her, as she struggled through evil to reach the source of good across the river.

The memory of the boy Alan, defying the Lord himself, gave her courage.

Just when she thought she was clear through, and would step out any moment into the bright sunlight, she heard it. That thin, cold voice with the trace of a lisp.

'Save the people,' it whispered against her ear. As she put

65

out a hand to protect herself, she touched the fur of the weasel, felt its tiny backbone, heard the murderous click of its needle teeth as it struck at her and missed.

'Save the people,' the Lord of the Moor jeered, and now she could see his eyes, very close to hers, hypnotic eyes that drained her will power.

'Save yourself,' he whispered. 'Save Rothe. Go back. Go ba-a-ack.' His voice was a thin echoing moan.

'Go back to hell!' she screamed. 'Favour!'

The mist cleared and there was nothing there but the bridge and the river, leaping and sparkling with points of light. As she went towards the bridge, she saw the grass above the river bank move in a ribbon of slithering movement as something very small and quick, like a weasel slipped away unseen.

The horse appeared to her like a fireball, and she climbed past the hollow in the rocks where Alan had sheltered his sheep, and joyfully on to his back, with no idea of where he would take her. She knew it would be something to do with Davey. Each time she flew with the horse, she hoped this would lead to the final solution, but she knew that there might be many journeys to make and many clues to unravel before her work was done.

A blast of deafening rock music hit her in the ears, and she was in a room where the music seemed to come out of the walls and the ceiling and the floor, so completely did it fill the space and fill the head of the person she had now become.

The person was dancing, twisting and turning and sticking bits of herself out in all directions. Her fat cheeks jounced. Her fat pink arms were like uncooked sausages. She moved her frenzied feet to the relentless beat, beat, beat.

It felt strange to Rose to be fat, as if your flesh was in charge of you, and you had to allow more space for yourself between the furniture.

'Oh yeah, oh yeah, oh yeah,' the girl howled.

66

The door opened, and an irate woman in an apron thundered in shouting, although you could only see her mouth opening widely, without hearing the words. She pushed Rose and the dancing girl aside and marched to the radio set and punched it into a stunned silence.

'Here, Gran.' The fat girl put her hands on her cushioned hips. 'Don't to that.'

'Shut up, Gwendolyn. I've been calling and calling, but you're too deaf or too stupid to hear. Go and see who's at the door.'

'You go.'

'It's no one for me,' the grandmother said, with the air of one who has been forgotten by life. 'One of your boy friends, if you can call that dopey creature a boy – or a friend.'

'Vernon?' Gwendolyn was a bit dopey herself. Rose, having access to the contents of her mind, could tell that there wasn't much in stock, and that her thinking mechanism ran as slowly as cold treacle.

Vernon was outside the door, with a droopy lip and a handful of dying wild flowers. He was weedy, like the flowers, shorter than Gwen, with a large head that ran up to a point from which his hair parted in the middle and fell on either side of his vacant face.

Gwen quite liked him, or at least she tolerated him, because he was dafter than she was, and she could control him. Gwen was sick of being controlled by her grandparents since her mother had walked out on her, and by teachers who tried to put her in special classes to learn home economics, when she knew she was going to be a rock star, and by her so-called friends at school who called her Whale, and had to be put up with because otherwise she would have no friends.

'Look what the cat brought in,' she said. She hooked Vernon by the back of the collar and hauled him into her grandmother's front hall, which bristled with coat racks and hat pegs and was hung with fearsome religious pictures of martyrs in great pain.

'For me?' She took the flowers and laid them on top of the

'Like my eyeshadow?'

frame of St Somebody being attacked by smiling lions in the Roman Coliseum. 'What's up then?' For somebody who needed friends, she had not got a very gracious manner.

'Hey,' said Vernon, 'you look all right today.'

'Like my eye shadow? "Riot," they call it.'

Vernon blinked, as if it dazzled him. When Gwendolyn moved to the mirror on the coatstand to check on 'Riot', Rose saw that it was lizard green with silver flecks. She saw that Gwen had a fat, lost sort of face, with a turned down

68

mouth and pale blue, confused eyes that looked as if they had seen trouble.

'Want to come in?'

Vernon shot a scared glance towards the closed door of the front room. 'Your gran home?'

'Don't mind her. We'll go in the back room and play some music, eh?'

'All right.'

Gwen was wondering if she could risk taking him to the kitchen to look for biscuits, when the door of the front room opened and her grandmother came out.

'Hullo, Vernon,' she said without enthusiasm. 'Did you come over by yourself?'

'Of course he did, Gran, what do you think? He's not daft.'

'Oh? Well I'm glad to hear that,' the grandmother said in the special, slow, patient voice she used on Gwendolyn when she was having one of her vague days.

'Well, I have to go now.' Vernon shifted the heavy boots at the end of his thin legs uncomfortably.

'Stay for tea,' Gwen said impulsively.

His lip dropped. His eyes rolled at the grandmother, who said, 'I'm sorry you can't stay, Vernon,' and went back into the front room.

'Why did you come then?' Gwen followed him to the front door.

'Dunno.' He turned and looked at her. 'Oh yes, I remember. Your birthday that we talked about, when my uncle said he'd take us to the pictures. You coming?'

'No,' Gwen said. 'I've got something to do on my birthday.'

'Why?'

''Cos.'

'With your gran?'

'No.'

'What?'

'Something.' Gwen could not remember.

69

'Oh.'

They stood in the open doorway and talked to each other in monosyllables for a bit. Then Vernon tried again. 'My uncle said he'd take us to the pictures on your birthday,' and Gwen said, 'I'll be busy,' and shut the door.

CHAPTER NINE

Gwen's birthday. That was the only possible clue. Otherwise, what was the point of Gwendolyn and poor simple Vernon? Favour would not have taken her to the house with the pictures of tormented martyrs for nothing.

Rose went over the conversation again and again, trying to puzzle out a clue, but the only definite fact that emerged was the birthday. 'Your birthday that we talked about,' Vernon had said. But when was it? Tomorrow? Next week? The week after? Was something going to happen to Davey Morgan to make him cry, and if so, what had Gwen the Whale got to do with it?

Rose brooded next day at school, and was useless. At the hotel, she broke a few more things than usual, was in trouble with Hilda for burning toast, and with Mrs Ardis for not listening to her knotted string of complaints against Mr and Mrs Crabbe – 'The Almighty knew what he was doing when he gave them that name' – the aunt and uncle of the bride, who had already moved into the hotel and were finding fault with everything.

They had wanted the wedding at the Empire Rooms, or nowhere, for that matter, because they had never thought that George King was good enough for Jean.

As the wedding drew near and Mollie became more frantic, Samson Flite the caterer became calmer. Sam was a gentle, slow-moving young man, with lazy, smiling eyes and a relaxed view of life. He had chosen to leave the rat race of business, and indulge in his hobby of cooking in a timbered cottage in Newcome Hollow by the sea. Things that ought to be done today could perfectly well wait until tomorrow, if he wanted to read or sit on the beach or take his boat out.

When it was time to decorate the bridal cake, Rose and

Mollie went early to his cottage to put on the first symbolic touches, for good luck.

The huge edifice of fruitcake had its marzipan layer on all three tiers, and was already covered with pure white icing, the top like a field of newly fallen snow waiting for someone to make tracks in.

'It breaks my heart to spoil it,' Mollie said, 'but here goes.'

There were to be little white and yellow crowns all round the edge, because the bride and groom would be Mr and Mrs King by the time they cut the cake. Sam, wearing a striped chef's apron over his pyjamas, gave Mollie the icing bag and she piped out a perfect crown.

'Now you, Rose,' Sam said, as Mollie handed her the bag. 'Squeeze and lift.'

As he said it, Rose heard quite clearly the sound of the child crying. With the pitiful, agonized sound came a vision of his small, puckish face screwed up in fear, the round eyes staring.

Her hand trembled.

'Oh look, you've mucked it up,' Sam said serenely. He scooped off the squashed sugar crown and put it in Rose's mouth. 'Have another go.'

'No, I can't. I'll mess it up again.'

'You won't. Try another,' Mollie said. 'It's your good luck to them.'

'I don't feel lucky.'

She felt left out and in the dark. Mr Vingo had gone, and Favour's journeys were too mysterious.

'Oh pooh,' said Sam. 'Don't be tempermental.'

'What's the matter?' Mollie asked, as they walked home under the clear blue unused sky of a new day. She sometimes had to ask that nowadays, when Rose was distracted, half in this world, half in the other.

'I'm all *right*.' That was what Rose usually answered.

'Well, I just thought . . .'

One day, I will tell you. Her mother deserved to be told, and she might even understand. She deserved to be told everything. But not yet. Not for ages and ages yet.

Mr Vingo came back before the wedding. The mother of Jean, the bride, had pleased him by asking him to play, and he was teaching Abigail the melody of 'I Dream of Jeannie with the Light Brown Hair', so that they could serenade the bride in a duet.

Abigail rode her bicycle home from school with Rose, to practise.

New guests had just arrived and Jim, the handyman, was mowing the lawn, so Mollie asked Rose to help carry their bags into the annexe, where they were putting people this week so as to leave space for wedding guests. Abigail went on up to Mr Vingo and the piano.

In the annexe lounge, Mr and Mrs Crabbe were talking to the bride's mother. When Rose came down from the bedroom, they asked her to make them a pot of tea. She wanted to say, 'Make it yourself,' because the annexe kitchen was really to let the guests be independent, not to be served by the staff.

As she was waiting for the kettle to boil, she heard the bride's mother talking about the wedding. What else? It would be talked to death before it ever happened. Too bad if Jean changed her mind at the last minute.

'A group,' she said. 'Wave Breaks, they call themselves. Everybody has them. Dr Bolger told me he heard them at Lady Rowan's charity affair, and they were superb.'

When she carried the tray to the lounge, Rose said bluntly, for it was the only way to say a thing that had to be said, 'About the music for the wedding.'

'It's all arranged. Wave Breaks. The Wood Briar Hotel will really swing.'

'I thought you'd asked Mr Vingo to play.'

'Oh well, that was just a vague idea. We never settled it. I mean,' she explained to the Crabbes, 'the man's a genius in his way, but people want something they can dance to.'

Rose put down the tray, pretending not to hear Mrs Crabbe say, 'You forgot the sugar.'

'None of us take it, Muriel.'

'I like to see a tray properly laid.'

Rose went to the kitchen and out of the back door and along the path across the two gardens and into the hotel. She went up the back stairs and tramped up the spiral stair and opened the door of the turret room.

'Where you been? We want you to hear us.'

'Guess what,' Rose said heavily. She hated to wipe the smile off Mr Vingo's face, but when you've got to say something, you've got to say it.

'The wedding's off?' Abigail asked.

'They've hired some outfit called Wave Breaks. They're going to have the dining-room tables moved out, and open the doors to the lounge, and have dancing.'

'Oh good,' Abigail said. 'Can we dance too, in our frilly aprons?'

'You don't get the point. They don't want Mr Vingo to play.'

'I hate them,' Abigail said.

'No, no.' Mr Vingo went on smiling. 'I was getting cold feet anyway, weren't you, Abigail?'

'Sure.'

Rose minded more than they did.

'Listen up,' Abigail said. 'We'll do you "Jeannie". Special performance. Last time on any stage.'

'And then will you play me –' Rose gave Mr Vingo a special look – 'that other tune?'

He must help her. She must get back to the horse and find out more about Gwen's birthday, and whether it really was the clue, and if so, what it meant.

'There's no other tune,' Abigail objected. '"Jeannie" is the only one we've been practising.'

'The tune,' Rose said firmly to Mr Vingo.

He pretended not to understand, but as he turned back to the piano she heard him murmur, 'Let's see, let's see. I

74

might vary the accompaniment just a fraction of an infinitesimal fragment . . .'

'Don't throw me off my stroke,' Abigail warned.

'You won't even notice.'

And she didn't. As they played, Mr Vingo wove a few notes of Favour's tune skilfully into the piano music, and at the same time, from below the turret room, came an unmistakable sound: the snort of a horse.

Behind the backs of the musicians, Rose went to the window. There below, waiting for her on the very patch of grass Jim Fisher had cut only a minute or two ago with the lawn mower, was the shimmering, miraculous horse.

The window was open. She was quickly through and on to the sloping roof below. She slid to the edge and from there she dangled on the gutter until her feet touched the verandah rail and she could push off from it straight on to Favour's back. As they rose in that strong, bounding take-off, Rose, clutching the mane with both hands, looked back and saw Jim and the mower at the far end of the lawn, already far below, and totally unaware that a miracle had happened within a few yards of him.

'Hold the door! Here, give us a chance, Fred. This thing's got a wonky wheel. It's a brute to turn.'

Whoever she was now, Rose could hear the man's querulous voice right by her head, but she could not see him. She could not see anything but the ceiling, in fact, for she was lying on her back on a very flat moving surface that felt suspiciously like a hospital trolley. She had ridden on one once when she had her tonsils and adenoids out.

A jerk, which hurt her left leg, then, 'Oops, dearie,' as the ceiling changed to the lighted roof of a large lift. 'You all right, Beverly?'

'Uh, huh.' She gritted her teeth. Her leg hurt quite a lot. It was fixed into some kind of strapped-down splint casing, and she could not move it.

'What you got there then, Joe?'

She turned her head. There was another man in the lift, dressed like a hospital porter in a loose green jacket and trousers, with a square green cotton cap perched high on his bushy hair.

'Fracture of left tibia,' the voice near her head announced importantly. 'Going down to Mr McDonald for repair.'

'Help! Let me out of here!' Rose shouted silently. She knew that some of her journeys might be scary, but she had not bargained for an operation. Suppose the anaesthetic knocked Beverly out, but left Rose awake, and feeling everything?

Beverly was afraid, but not panicking. Her mind and vision were a little hazy, and a small sore spot in the bend of her elbow showed Rose that she had been given some kind of a sedative injection.

When she lifted her arm to look at it, Rose saw that the skin was very dark. How interesting. She had always wondered what it felt like to be black. Now she knew. It felt the same as being white.

The lift went smoothly down.

'How's the family?' Fred asked Joe.

'The usual. The kids drive me out of my mind a lot of the time, but the wife says I'm out of it anyway.'

'What can you do?' Fred laughed, as if he knew kids. And wives.

'They're good little beggars really, all things considered. Going to take 'em to the fun fair when it gets here.'

'That'll cost you.'

'The older ones can pay their way. That eldest boy of mine, he earns more after school than I do in this dump.'

Beverly and Rose did not like to hear the place to which they had entrusted their broken leg described as a dump, but the lift had stopped and the door opened. They rolled down a corridor under strip fluorescent lighting, past many doors, before they were wheeled into a room where a nurse in a green cap and surgical mask came forward at once, smiling with her eyes.

'Hullo, Beverly. Don't be scared. Everything's going to be just fine.'

'I'll say, "So long," then.' Joe came from the head of the trolley and patted Beverly's shoulder. He was a small man with a creased expression of worry under the green cotton cap he wore low on his forehead. When he smiled at her, however, the loose skin and creases of his face rearranged themselves into the flexible grin of a comedian, and his eyes twinkled.

'Just don't go climbing out of no windows no more,' he said, 'and you'll be all right.'

'I didn't,' Beverly said in a small scared voice, because she saw a white-clad doctor approaching. 'Fell off my bike.'

Why had Joe said, 'climbing out of a window'? There was no way he could have known that Rose was an observer of this whole scene, nor how she had got here.

Before she could puzzle out Joe's involvement with the mysterious rearrangement of time and space which the horse had made possible, Joe was gone and the doctor was by her side, tying a rubber tube round her upper arm and telling her to make a fist.

Beverly felt a bit weepy. The sedative had weakened her resolve to go through this ordeal with the heart of a lion, as she had promised her father.

'Leg hurt you?'

She nodded, licking at a tear.

'We'll fix that up in no time,' the young doctor said cheerily. 'When you wake up, you'll be as good as new.'

While he was talking, he had inserted the needle deftly into her vein without her feeling more than a prickle.

'Now a luv-ver-ly sleep,' he said softly. 'I want you to count for me, Beverly, backwards from ten, can you do that, there's a love. Come on, ten, nine . . .'

'Eight, seven, si-six . . .' Beverly's voice faded away into nothing and she floated peacefully into unconsciousness.

* * *

'I'll never play the flute for you again, never. So just try and ask me and she where it gets you.'

Abigail was leaning out of the turret room window. Rose was sitting on the lawn by the corner verandah, wondering if she would be able to put weight on her left leg when she stood up.

'Jim shouted.' She had to think quickly.

'Why? It had better be a good answer. That's twice you've run out on me.'

'He caught his finger in the throttle lever. I had to get to him quickly. He's all right now.'

Jim was mowing the lawn in parallel strips of light and dark, the grass bending different ways as he changed direction. Last year, he did once catch his finger in the throttle, and had to be rescued by Philip Wood, so it was not quite a lie.

'Neat way to come down.' Abigail waved goodbye to Mr Vingo and climbed out of the window and down the roof, and dropped to the rail and then the ground, one-handed, carrying her flute case.

'By the way,' Rose asked Abigail before she went home, 'When is the fun fair coming?'

'I don't know. Is it?'

'It's supposed to. Shall we go?'

'Maybe.'

Hearing Joe mention the fun fair might have been a clue, and the reason for Rose being Beverly in the hospital and almost having an operation. But so might broken legs, bicycles, low pay for hospital porters. How were any of these tied up with danger to little Davey?

Mr Vingo's head appeared above, blocking the whole window opening.

'Sorry you had to leave.' He smiled down at Rose, his cheeks pouchy, his treble chins resting like bolsters on the window sill. 'Everything all right?'

'I hope so.'

'You got his finger free,' Abigail said.

'I hope it won't happen again. It's tricky.' Rose tilted her head up to Mr Vingo.

'I know.' He chuckled. 'But with stubborn patience, you'll meet the challenge.'

'Buying a new lawn mower would be better,' Abigail said.

CHAPTER TEN

Rose loved her father and he loved her.

If he and Mollie were only to have one child, he would have liked a boy. Rose understood that. When she was small, she followed him about with a pocketful of nails, banging away with a small hammer and learning things about carpentry and measuring and painting, and helping him in his workshop.

Now she more often worked with Mollie in the hotel, and although the love and the good strong memories of her childhood were still there between her and her father, neither of them could find ways to express it.

Lately it seemed, if one of them reached out – 'Want to come up to the stables and see me ride in the gymkhana, Dad?' or, 'Come down to the lab with me some time, and I'll show you why tea bags are a peril to the human stomach' – the other one perversely would not respond.

'Too busy,' or, 'Another time,' or, 'You do it then tell me about it,' or, 'I can't, Dad, I've got oodles to do.'

Rose often kicked herself when she turned him down, or got angry at one of his rotten jokes, and she wondered if he kicked himself too, when he was sarcastic or indifferent to her. If so, they were a pair of fools, because it would have been easier to be nice to each other, as Mollie sometimes reminded them.

So when her father asked her if she would like to go to the Kitchen and Catering Fair with him, Rose was going to say, 'It's too near the wedding, I won't have time,' but she quickly switched to, 'Thanks, I'd love it.'

'Wear something decent, for God's sake. I'll have clients there.'

Philip Wood was going to the Kitchen Fair to look at

new gadgets. His job was quality testing for small manufacturers and for a consumer magazine that told its readers which appliances and food and cosmetics were the best to buy, and which were second rate, or were actually bad for you.

Being a rather negative person, the kind who would say a money box was half empty, instead of half full, he did not mind telling people that things they liked would do them no good. It did not seem to make much difference anyway. They went on ruining themselves in their own way.

Hot dogs were one way. As part of the magazine's campaign against junk food, Philip Wood and an analyst had proved without a doubt that the skin in some brands was highly questionable, and that the filling had been known to contain items that you would not normally buy for food. Yet you could not go to any public place where people were gathered without seeing them selling – like hot dogs.

They were selling them in a snack bar at the Kitchen Fair, although many of the exhibits were for gourmet cooking, or were health foods. Rose left her father talking to people at the stand for growing lettuces in water, and dodged aside to the snack bar and bought herself a savoury dog, slathered with fiery hot mustard. She walked off in the opposite direction, so that he would not have the pain of seeing her eat it.

Kitchen Fair . . . Fun Fair. Who was that hospital porter? Or was it Beverly who could provide the clue? Rose walked thoughtfully along the crowded aisle between the exhibits. How could she get the horse to take her back to the Morgan family, so that she could get a better idea of where their house might be?

Once when she got out of school early, she had bicycled into Newcome and had hunted again in likely places for the house in that dishevelled street. On the train journey up here with her father, she had stood in the corridor staring down at the terraces and blocks of flats and small factories and junk yards that they passed before the train drew away into the open country. Nothing looked anything like that derelict dead-end street.

Perhaps it was not even in Newcome. Perhaps it was in this big city where she was roaming about in an exhibition hall full of strangers, eating a hot dog. Perhaps that was why she had not turned down her father's invitation this time. The horse had ordained that she would accept nicely, and she would be rewarded.

She turned round and went back for another hot dog. Thinking deeply always made her hungry.

'Rose Wood, what are you doing?'

It was a man with a motheaten beard and fanatical eyes: her father's friend who had invented the newfangled tin opener.

'I came with my father.'

'No, I mean, with a hot dog. Your father would have a fit.'

'He won't know.'

'Here he is.' He turned her round, away from her father's approach. 'Listen Phil,' he greeted Philip Wood, 'it's the greatest good luck finding Rose here. I'm having a bit of a problem with Eezeeduzzit. The woman the agency sent to demonstrate it has cut her finger, and –'

'On the tin opener?' Rose's father looked amused.

'No, no – well, in a way, I suppose, but it was her own fault. I sent her to First Aid, but it doesn't look too good to have a tin opener with the slogan, "So Simple a Child Can Use It" demonstrated by a grown-up with a whopping great bandage on her finger with blood leaking through. Then I saw Rose.' His inventive eyes gleamed. 'And I realized, ha, ha, she's saved the day! If Eezeeduzzit is so simple a child can use it – right, we'll use a child to demonstrate it.'

Rose did not know what to say. She looked at her father.

'It would be against the law to employ a minor here,' he said rather pompously.

'Oh no, no, not for pay. I mean, not that Rose wouldn't be worth it, but just for fun, and as a favour. Would you,

82

Rose?' He made his face very sad and his eyes lost their gleam. 'To tell you the truth, I'm having a bit of trouble interesting people in my marvellous device. It's hard to get sales, and what with the rent of the booths going up this year – oh dear.' He sighed.

'I'll try, if you like,' Rose said. After all, if she had joined Favour in his crusade to help people in trouble, she couldn't very well turn down other people who came her way under their own steam.

'Can I, Dad?' she remembered to ask.

'Not if the damn thing's going to cut your finger.'

'It couldn't,' his friend said, 'and listen, Phil, you're not to write something terrible about Eezeeduzzit in that magazine of yours. The woman cut her finger on the tin, not on the opener.'

It was a rather complicated electrical device. You needed to press a switch and two buttons in a certain order, but if you got it right, it whipped the lids off soup tins and baked beans, and even unscrewed jars.

Rose felt rather foolish sitting at a table out in front of the booth with an Eezeeduzzit and a stack of tins. She was supposed to ask passers-by, 'May I show you our magic opener?' but after she had risked that with two or three people who had walked on as if she did not exist, she left the inventor to do the talking.

Having mastered the knack of the Eezeeduzzit, Rose kept ripping off lids, but the back of the booth was piling up with opened tins – no one could possibly eat that many baked beans – and they were running out of new ones. She could only demonstrate the opener if someone stopped at her table.

It was fun when people stopped. Rose enjoyed showing off her skill. And it did take some skill. Visitors who tried it for themselves almost always failed the first few times. A husband who was looking for a birthday present for his wife tried ten times, and only mangled the top of a tin of celery soup.

'So simple, a child can use it,' its inventor kept chanting to the uncaring crowds, and the husband thrust the humming device away from him and said bitterly, 'It *takes* a child to use it.'

'Perhaps your wife would rather not have something for the kitchen anyway,' Rose said helpfully, 'since it's her birthday.'

When they got into the train to go home, Rose left her bag of samples from the various stalls on the seat and went to stand in the corridor again, telling her father she was stiff from sitting in the table at the booth.

She was on the opposite side of the line now, and she looked very carefully as they pulled out of the city station, straining her eyes through the dusk for shabby streets that ended at the railway, until the train gathered speed and the streets and rows of houses began to wheel by too fast.

She went back into the carriage and sat down.

'Had a good time?' her father asked.

'Lovely. Thanks.'

She had liked being among the crowd at the Fair, and seeing all the different exhibits, and tasting the food and weird fizzy drinks and cocoa made without chocolate.

When she was demonstrating Eezeeduzzit, and answering questions and hearing people say things like, 'Look, Harold, that's a lot better than that rusty old thing we've got,' she had felt part of the bustling world of commerce. It was all very real and practical.

She settled down to go through her bag of samples and pamphlets, and compare them with her father's bag. They chatted away like colleagues, discussing lists of ingredients and extravagant claims for this and that – 'Never scrub a saucepan again!', taking critical bites of each other's health food bars, worrying what Mollie would think of their gifts for her. Now that she was an official demonstrator for Eezeeduzzit, Rose took a professional interest in the varying merits and uselessness of the gadgets.

When they were near Newcome, she did not want to have to go into the corridor again, to study the streets on this side of the line. She did not want to have to keep worrying about Davey Morgan, whoever he was. She wanted just to be ordinary Rose Wood, returning from an afternoon out with her father.

The train slowed, then stopped. A woman in the carriage stood up and began to pull bags down from the rack. A jerk forward, and she sat down again with a bump. The train hooted, a sad wail, and at the point where the noise of the hooter began to trail off into the night sky, the crying of the child moved in to take its place, and remind Rose that she could not be ordinary any more.

As she followed her father's long stride out to the car park, she saw that they were passing a line of posters that advertised, FUN FAIR! FUN FAIR! FUN FAIR!

CHAPTER ELEVEN

The day before the wedding, everything looked promising. The bridegroom's parents, a jolly, square couple from the North, arrived and were thrilled with everything. They called Mollie 'My dear' and Rose 'Love', and made their own beds and cleaned the bath, and made friends with all the other guests, and did not seem to notice that the Crabbes, the bride's aunt and uncle, were not making friends with them.

Their daughter Alice, who was about Rose's age, was to be one of the bridesmaids. Her long flowered cotton voile dress was on a hanger in her room, with a pair of white sandals standing neatly beneath it.

The night before the wedding, Rose was woken by the sound of hurrying feet along an upper corridor. A door banged. A telephone rang. Someone ran down the stairs. A car door shut, the engine started, and gravel scattered as it was pulled fast out of the car park.

Early on the wedding morning, the news was all over the hotel. Not only was it raining, but the bridegroom's sister Alice had been taken ill and was now in the hospital, minus her appendix.

Mrs King came back to the hotel and wept, because she had had a bad night and could not bear to think either of her Alice recovering from the operation in the hospital, nor of the lovely flowered dress she had made herself with such care, hanging forlornly above the politely waiting sandals.

The bride was upset about the spoiling of her plans. She could not come to the hotel, because George was there comforting his parents, and it was bad luck to see him before she walked up the aisle to him in church. Her mother came, in paint-stained jeans and an old sweater, her long grey hair tied back with a rubber band, as if it wasn't only a few hours before she would be Mother of the Bride – elegantly dressed, Mrs Crabbe hoped – in the left front pew.

'Happy the bride the sun shines on,' she said with an ironic grimace, shaking rain out of her hair. 'Jeannie is terribly upset, poor darling. I mean–' she nodded at the Kings – 'she's sorry for poor Alice, of course, but it does seem a shame, when she planned it all so carefully.'

Rose brought her a cup of coffee, and Mr King, who normally kept quiet while the women talked, suddenly cried, 'Got it!'

'Got what?' Mrs Crabbe asked suspiciously.

'Rose, of course. Just the ticket, aren't you, love? Let her understudy for our Alice. There's your bridesmaid.'

'Oh, but I . . .' Rose stepped backwards in response to a strong urge to escape.

'You mean, wear the flower wreath and the dress and everything?' the bride's mother asked. 'She wouldn't be the right size.'

'Why not? All young girls are the same size,' said Mr King, who was not very observant, and his wife said, 'We'll make it fit. That's a wonderful idea. Would you, Rose love?'

'Well, I . . .'

'Please do it, Rose.' The bride's mother smiled warmly at her, and held out her hands. 'Jeannie will be so pleased. You'll save the day.'

Mollie was delighted. 'If you want to do it, Rose.'

'I do and I don't. There's a lot of work to do.'

'We'll manage. Come on, let's go up and try on the dress.'

It was a bit tight in the waist and shoulders, but Rose sucked in her stomach in front of the long mirror in her mother's room, and had to admit that she looked all right.

The florist had brought a wreath of real flowers for her hair, and she carried a small bouquet, which matched the pale yellow and tawny flowers on the white background of the dress.

Abigail knelt to fasten the strap of the tight sandals, which would be giving her hell in a few hours, and put another hairpin in the wreath.

'Gee.' She stepped back and looked at Rose's reflection, then turned her round so she could look at the real thing. '*You . . . look . . . swell*,' she said, with deep satisfaction.

Rose did all right at the church. She did not drop the bouquet. She did not trip over the bride's train, or her own feet. When she walked back down the aisle on the arm of the best man, she could hear people whispering to each other, 'Who is that? That's not Alice. Who's that?'

Rose grinned at them. A woman of mystery.

When Jean and George stepped out of the church doorway, the rain had stopped and the sun was out in a sky full of hurrying clouds. The wind blew her veil up high and she looked as if she were going to take off and fly into married life.

At the hotel, Rose escaped to the kitchen and put an apron over the bridesmaid's dress and started to help Hilda.

'Where's the bridesmaid? Where's Rose?'

She had to go out again for the photographs, just remembering in time to take off her apron. Then she went back to Hilda and Jim in the kitchen, which already looked as if a bomb had gone off in it.

When Wave Breaks started to play, Rose took off her apron again and came through the hall to watch the new Mr and Mrs George King circle the floor alone in a waltz, before other dancers joined in.

After the cutting of the magnificent cake, she was going to nip upstairs and change into her white blouse and skirt and frilly apron, so that she could help Abigail to hand round cake, and pack pieces of it in little silver boxes for people to take home. Wave Breaks were doing some Country and Western music. One of the guitarists had a fiddle, and he began to saw it upwards into the unmistakable phrasing, the light soaring notes, always strange

'You . . . look . . . swell,' said Abigail.

each time, but always familiar. Rose knew that the horse was calling her.

Not now. I'm at a wedding.

Some people were dancing a kind of polka, kicking up their heels to the fiddler's jig, but the fiddler persisted in sliding up into Favour's tune at the end of each chorus. Rose had to turn away and move like a sleepwalker towards the back door by the boots and coats passage, where nobody would see her.

Outside, she picked up her skirt and ran. Half way through the wood, she took off the slipping wreath and hung it on the branch of a tree. At the wall of the sheep pasture, she took off the sandals and left them on top of the stones and ran across the wet turf in her bare feet, which were still tough from going without shoes in the summer.

It was hard to run in the long dress. She could not hold it up all the time. The bottom got soaked and muddy, and gorse bushes snatched at it. Going through the thicket at the edge of the lake, brambles made a grab for the sash and tore it away, as Rose hurried on.

The lake was gone. The valley was there below her in the mist. The soldiers were there somewhere. She could hear them talking and laughing. Would the Lord of the Moor be there too? Oh God, if the Lord appeared in front of her, with the smell of evil coming from him like a deadly poison, she was afraid that she would turn and run.

Which was she more afraid of – confronting the Lord, or turning back from the horse's summons? Something slid across her bare foot. She screamed and stopped her sliding descent. If the weasel was there, the Lord was somewhere near. But the horse was ahead, and if she turned back now he might abandon her, and she would never see him again.

'What happens to messengers who don't to their job?' she had once asked Mr Vingo. He had shuddered and answered, 'Don't even ask me. I not only don't know, but I can't imagine anything so horrible.'

Standing still, balancing on the slope, Rose strained her

eyes into the mist, and listened with all her senses alert. Nothing. Faintly, like a scent brought on a gust of wind, then gone, the smell of unwashed men and burned meat and horses and manure of the castle courtyard. She moved on.

'Save the people!'

The Lord's whisper stopped her heart. The touch of his chill fingers on the back of her neck sent her crashing forward, stumbling and slipping, her spine crawling with the fear that he would catch her. When she broke out into the sunlight at last, she felt that it was just in time.

She was gasping for breath as she climbed up to the horse. He bent his neck to her, and his grey eye was mild, as if he was smiling. Of course she would never turn back! There was no choice. When she had climbed, rather awkwardly because of the dress, on to his back, the fear was gone. The other side of the valley, still tyrannized by the Lord and his men, was a world away. They could not reach or harm her. Nothing could touch her, because she was where she belonged on the back of this powerful spirit-horse, who bore her away joyfully into the sky.

And so I said to him, "Mr Tompkins," I said, "promises is all very well, but promises won't put a roof over my children's heads, and broken promises from the Housing Department I don't want to hear no more of. You'll have to see my husband.'"

Oh good. Rose was back at the Morgans. She was Carol again, in clothes that were too small for her, riding a very ancient bone-shaking bicycle with a flat back tyre. The loud voice came through an open window of the house where Linda and Susan had heard Davey crying. Carol turned her bicycle through the gateway whose gate had fallen off, and before she got off and went to the back door, Rose saw again the dark mouth of the pedestrian tunnel in the high brick wall. Why had she missed this street when she had looked so hard from the train?

'What did he say?' Mr Morgan was sitting with his wife at

the kitchen table, with a pot of tea and a loaf of bread between them.

"'I'll see your husband," he said.' Mrs Morgan had Davey on her lap and was feeding him spoonfuls of sugar wetted with tea from her cup. 'You'll have to give it to him straight and strong, Joe.'

Mr Morgan did not look as if he could give anything straight and strong to the Housing Department. He was smaller and weaker than his wife, almost bald, with a creased, gnome-like smile. Rose did not recognize him at first without his baggy green trousers and jacket and the square cotton hat. Then she realized. Joe. The other hospital porter had called him that.

'Hullo Mum, hullo Dad, hullo my little Davey.' Carol took a mug without a handle from the sink, rinsed it sketchily, sat down at the table on a chair with no back that could now be called a stool, and reached for the teapot.

Her mother cut her a hunk of bread, and her father pushed the jampot over.

'Where's the butter?'

'Where's the butter, she wants to know,' Mrs Morgan informed Davey, who said, 'Where bu'er' and beat a spoon on the table and threw it at one of the cats.

'You've not seen butter in this house, girl, since your Dad got laid off at the printing works. Part time at that butcher's shop hospital isn't going to put even marge on the table, the way the price of everything is going up.'

'Any biscuits?' Carol asked cheerfully.

'Any biscuits, she says.' When she yelled hoarsely in his ear, Davey slid off her vast lap and waddled round the table to climb on Carol's knee. She kissed the top of his head and he turned up a jammy, beaming face and said, 'Davey love Carol.'

She hugged him tightly, while her mother's voice went on. 'When you're in work and bringing money home, then you can talk about butter and biscuits. Until then, do me a favour and shut up.'

Although she talked roughly to all the family, including Joe, they understood that it was as normal as breathing to her. If she had ceased the non-stop harangue, they would have missed the secure familiarity of this noisy, energetic, powerfully loving mother.

Rose stayed with Carol at the Morgan's house for the rest of the day. She worried that the wedding would be over before she got back, until she remembered that in all her journeys, time in the real world stood still, and she returned at the same time as she had left, quicker even than the briefest dream. But there was the run to the lake and back. That took real time. She would have to get back to Wood Briar in time to throw the confetti when Jean and George left on their honeymoon.

As Carol, she went upstairs to the unmade bed, which had a damp spot from Davey's nap, and wrote an essay for her English teacher, entitled, 'Winter in Newcome'.

Rose was very excited when Carol wrote this at the top of the page. Now she knew for sure which town this street and this house were in. Carol got quite excited too, because she liked writing. Her imagination took off like a train, stringing words together and pulling them along. Rose, who wrote slowly and with difficulty, loved the feeling of Carol's hand moving steadily across the paper, the words seeming to come by themselves. She liked the tension in Carol's body as she leaned forward, cramped over the writing pad, with her hair falling in her eyes and her breath coming fast, oblivious to everything but the world of winter she was capturing on the page.

When she had finished, she sighed deeply and said, 'If you don't like *that*, Miss Corcoran, I'll kill you.' Then she got off the bed and lifted a loose floorboard and took out of the space underneath a thin pile of papers. She took them back to the bed, because there was nowhere else to sit down, found an empty page and began to write a poem.

When the people go away
And the shops on the front are shuttered and cold
And the sea lashes at the legs of the pier like ice dragons
    of fury
And the snow falls at the sea's edge and melts and be-
    comes the sea
And is drawn away into the cold ocean
To break on the shores of warm lands far away,
Then my heart is cold and shuttered too
Because my love is gone.
But the spring will unlock my despair and then
My heart will fly away to join him in the warm lands.

Carol wrote the whole poem without pausing. It just
poured out of her. Rose was amazed and impressed. Now
that she knew how it was done, she would write a poem to
the Great Grey Horse, and Mr Vingo could set it to music
and put it into the next bit of his Ballad of Favour.

Carol went downstairs dreamily, and was shouted at by
her mother for mooning about upstairs.

'I was doing my homework,' she said virtuously. 'Like
you said to do.'

'Well, it can't take you all night. I need you to peel spuds
for the chips, and then you've got to go to the shop, if I can
find where I put the mug with the cash.'

'Why can't Mavis peel spuds?'

''Cos it's not my job, it's yours,' Mavis shouted from the
room across the passage.

'Who says?'

'I do.'

Carol leaped across the passage and pounced on Mavis,
who was lying on the bed-settee watching television and
filing her nails. They fought and struggled, until Mavis fell
on to the floor, waving the nail file and crying, 'I'll stab
you!'

Carol pulled her ankle away just in time. Mr Morgan
who was trying to watch the News, pushed at Mavis with

the toe of his small shoe and said feebly, 'Be a good girl now.'

'Why?'

He shrugged his shoulders. His children were beyond him.

Carol stood the five-year-old boy Gregory on a chair by the sink to peel the potatoes with a blunt knife. Then she put little Davey into the push chair and walked to the off-licence and grocery a few streets away for a packet of soap powder and a bottle of beer for her father.

'We don't serve minors,' the man behind the counter said, while at the same time leaning over to drop a bottle of beer in a brown paper bag into the torn carrier at the back of the push chair.

In the streets, Rose kept looking at everything to see if she could find a landmark. There were no church steeples or high buildings, but she did see, several streets away, the back of a large hoarding, just the legs and struts. She could not see what it advertised, but it might help.

As they came back to the house, a small shunting engine passed very slowly across the viaduct above the brick wall.

'Look, Davey!' Carol picked him out of the chair and held him up to see the top of the engine passing along above the wall. 'Choo choo train.'

'Saw choo choo.' He ran into the kitchen and grabbed the leg of his mother, who was frying chips.

'Did you, my angel? There's a clever boy.'

'He couldn't have. There's been none on that branch line for years,' Arthur said. 'What have you been putting into his head, Carol?'

'He saw an engine.'

'Going where?'

'How should I know?'

'I thought you were supposed to know everything.'

'I know more than you, and that's no great strain.'

'Knock it off. You give me a pain.'

That was a fair sample of the conversation in this family.

They threw insults back and forth at each other, but nobody seemed to mind.

Carol sat Davey in his wobbly high chair, which was covered in grease and jam and congealed egg and porridge. His father gave him a sip of beer. His mother put some chips and a spoonful of salt in front of him on the grubby linoleum tablecloth, and he ate contentedly.

He was wet and grimy and they fed him all the wrong things, but he was healthy and much loved. If anything were to happen to him, they would be desolated, and Carol would never get over it.

Supper wasn't much. A few eggs scrambled between them, a mountain of chips, and Arthur had brought home some of yesterday's cakes from the place where he worked. Rose wanted to go back to her own life. She had a landmark now. She knew she had been looking in the wrong place, near the main railway line, instead of this old abandoned branch line in a completely different part of Newcome.

She wanted to get back to the wedding. She concentrated hard. She held her breath. She tried to make Carol feel sleepy. But she had no effect on Carol, with her lively mind and quick tongue, who did not feel like going to bed for hours.

When Carol took Davey up to put him to sleep on the damp side of the bed she shared with him and Gregory, he pointed to the window and cried out something unintelligible.

'What did you see?' Carol looked out. 'There's nothing there. Just the sheet blowing in the wind.'

'Fly?' Davey asked hopefully.

'Did it look like a big bird flying?' Carol knelt down and hugged him. 'Ooh, you are a bright little beggar. Perhaps you'll grow up to be a poet, like me.'

When Rose saw him tucked up in the bed, a dark shudder of foreboding gripped her. She wanted to tell Carol, '*Don't leave him here. He's in danger.*'

'You're all right, aren't you, ducky?' Carol and Davey

exchanged a messy kiss and she stepped carefully over the loose floorboard and went whistling down the stairs.

'Get the wash in, will you?' her mother shouted.

'Only because I want a breath of fresh air anyway.'

Outside in the dark, Rose tried to imagine that the flapping sheet was the grey horse, prancing restlessly and swinging his heavy tail. Carol leaned into it to subdue it while she took out the pegs, and Rose was smothered in the sheet. It wound itself about her and took her breath away.

CHAPTER TWELVE

When she found herself back on the moor in the bedraggled bridesmaid's dress, Rose ran in her bare feet as fast as she could to Wood Briar.

She picked the sandals from the wall and carried them, and picked the wreath off the tree as she ran through the wood. She slipped through the back door and up the back stairs to her own room. There she changed into her waitress clothes, banged a brush into her wet, tangled hair and ran downstairs with a bright smile.

'Where you *been*?' Abigail was helping Sam to clear off the buffet. 'Mr Vingo said you'd gone away because you felt sick, but no one could find you.'

'I'm OK. Here, where's another tray? I'll help.'

'Rose, where *have* you been? I've been so worried.' Mollie turned her round to look into her face. 'I looked everywhere for you.. What's the matter? Are you all right? Too much rich food?'

'Don't blame the food,' Sam warned. 'Too much champagne, would it be?'

'Half a glass to toast the bride, that's all I had. Leave me alone, everybody. I'm all right. I felt dizzy and I went out to get some fresh air, that's all.'

'Too much excitement,' her father said, coming in on the end of the conversation. 'I knew no good would come of it all.'

'You sound like Mrs Crabbe.' Mollie looked round quickly to make sure the pessimistic aunt was not within hearing. 'It's been a beautiful wedding. So romantic, don't you think? Jeannie's a lovely girl, and they're very much in love. It takes me back.'

'To those long ago days when you used to be in love with me?' Philip asked.

'Idiot. I still am.' She kissed him.

'I love you too,' he said slowly and seriously.

It must be the champagne. He never said that to Rose's mother – at least, not when anyone could hear.

'No time for fooling.' He restored his old self again. 'The bride's ready to go, thank God, and she's going to chuck her bouquet over the stairs, for some peculiar reason.'

'So that all the unmarried women like us can fight for it.' Abigail put down her tray, patted her hair, which was folded in a chignon, licked a finger and ran it over her tidy eyebrows. 'Whoever catches it, they'll be married before the year is out.'

Rose and Abigail and two or three little girls and the other young women who were at the wedding were gathered in the hall when Jean appeared at the top of the stairs in her red going-away suit.

'Good luck!' she called, and hurled her flowers into the air, their white ribbons streaming.

The hands went up to grab. Bodies knocked into each other. There was a scramble, and Rose found herself on the floor, holding the flowers.

'Yay, Rose!' Abigail cheered her. Everyone clapped. Rose got up, feeling the warmth of a blush spreading up from her neck.

'Who's the lucky fellow?' people called out, and other witty things designed to embarrass a person. Then their attention switched to Jean and George, and everyone went outside and threw confetti and rice at them, as they ducked to the car and drove away, with Jean's brother and some of the children running after it down the road.

'Thanks for saying I felt sick,' Rose grabbed Mr Vingo and pulled him off round the side of the hotel while the crowd was going back inside. 'You saved my neck.'

'Well, I knew where you'd gone,' he said.

'Could you hear the tune too?'

'I guessed at it. I can't hear it as clearly as you can, except when I play it for you myself. But I knew you were hearing it.'

'Because I disappeared?'

'Before that. Because of your face.'

'What about it?'

'It had left us before you did.'

'I've found out a lot of things.' They walked round to the back of the hotel. Mr Vingo looked tired and pale. His hair was untidy. His bow tie was crooked. 'Clues, you know. But a bit disjointed. Why does Favour make it so hard to see where things fit?'

'Because he's only a horse, after all. He can only take you to the scenes and trust you to put it all together and know what to do.'

'What I've got to do is find these people now. The child's in danger. I don't know how or when, but I think I've got to warn them. It's funny. I've been with this family twice now, as one of them, so I know them quite well, but now I've got to go and meet them as Rose, a stranger. Want to come with me?'

'I can't, Rose a stranger, Rose of all roses. It has to be you. That's the way it works.'

'It's a lonely game,' Rose said.

'It's the only game,' Mr Vingo said.

'We're lucky, aren't we?'

'You can say that again.' He had been picking up some of Abigail's expressions.

Rose did not feel so lucky when Mrs King discovered the state of the bridesmaid's dress. She was leaving tomorrow, to stay nearer the hospital, and she asked Rose to bring the dress to her room so that she could pack it.

Rose knocked on the door and went in, with the dress on her arm and the sandals dangling from her hand. She had folded the dress so that the worst tears and stains would not show.

Mrs King was in a plaid dressing-gown, her body bulging all over the place in relief at being let out of the tight satin suit. An open suitcase was on the bed. Rose stepped forward and was going to put the folded dress into it, but Mrs King took it from her.

'I'll pack it. I'm a champion folder.' She shook out the dress, and gave a short, loud scream.

'I'm sorry,' Rose mumbled, swinging the sandals against her legs in great embarrassment. 'It got a bit dirty. I'll pay for the cleaning.'

'Got a bit dirty – it's ruined!' Mrs King stood there with her feet planted wide apart under the dressing-gown, holding up the dress. Then she gathered it to her and hugged it as if it were a wounded child. 'My Alice's dress, that I trusted you with. And Alice lying there in pain in that hospital bed while you went gallivanting about in her beautiful gown.'

'Well, here, wait a minute.' Rose stopped being embarrassed and became angry. 'I never asked to be part of the wedding. You were the ones who begged me to. I only did it to help out.'

Mrs King gave another short, loud scream. She had just seen the white sandals, which were now mottled brown and green from earth and wet grass. She snatched the wretched sandals from Rose and wrapped them hastily in newspaper, as if they were indecent. The dress lay limply on the bed. As she turned to mourn over it again, her third scream made Rose retreat to the doorway and half way out of the room.

'The sash! You've lost the sash. Oh, Rose, you *silly* girl!'

'I'm sorry.' Rose could not say, 'It's caught up in the brambles at Noah's Bowl,' so she went out and shut the door, and escaped to her room. She felt bad about the dress, but with what she had on her mind she had not got the time to sympathize with Mrs King.

On Sunday, Rose went off to Newcome before the Kings came down to breakfast. She did not want to be there if the whole thing started up again. Hilda and Gloria and Mrs Ardis had begun to clean up, and were all rather grumpy and discouraged, now that the excitement of the wedding was over and they had nothing to look forward to. But

Rose's excitement was still to come. She was on the brink of her own great adventure of rescue. The goings-on at Wood Briar seemed oddly tame and irrelevant.

First she had to warn the Morgans that Davey was in danger. She found her way to the part of town where the old branch line led to what used to be an area of small factories, until most of them failed, for one reason or another, and went out of business. There was an ancient, dank canal here, and at one point the branch line rose to cross it. This might be where she would find the brick railway viaduct with the tunnel.

Keeping the railway in sight, Rose looked in vain for the back of the hoarding, raised above a flat roof on its iron struts. A big advertisement for a car hire firm kept catching her eye – 'WHY PAY MORE?' – with a grotesque picture of a grinning family packing themselves into a small silver car, plus the grinning dog. 'ENJOY MILES GALORE!'

She put a foot on the ground to stop the bicycle, and looked at the sign again. Of course. Stupid Rose. '*Silly* girl.' (The thought of Mrs King gave her a small pang of guilt, but not too troublesome). This was the front of the hoarding of which she had seen the back.

She rode through some streets until she could see the back of it from the same angle, and – Oh, my God, there was the off-licence grocer's shop where the man who didn't serve minors served beer to minors for their fathers. It was the strangest feeling to see it as herself, having seen it in her disembodied state, when the only body she had was Carol's.

Here was the high kerb up which Carol had tipped the front wheels of the push chair. Here was the piece of pavement by the window full of soup tins and faded cake mix packets where Carol had made Rose anxious by deciding to leave Davey while she went inside, before she glanced up the street and saw a jostling line of boys, and changed her mind and pushed him into the shop.

And here was the corner which led to the way to the Morgan's house.

Rose got off and wheeled her bicycle, rather slowly now, because she was rehearsing what she was going to say. She turned the corner and walked down the street of shabby houses where Carol had walked, singing to Davey while she pushed him with one hand, her head high and the other hand making theatrical gestures to an imaginary audience. Another corner. Rose stopped and sighed deeply, partly with relief, partly to fill herself with oxygen for the undertaking.

Here was the deserted street at last, and there was the Morgan's house. There was the gate lying on the ground. There was the window with the dying plants through which Carol had gazed and daydreamed. There was the house across the street, with the cat in the window box again. There was the shadowy entrance to the tunnel.

There was Carol's old wreck of a bicycle, leaning against the wall under the kitchen window. There was the front door, with the pram without wheels blocking it. No good knocking on that door. Rose had never seen anyone go in or out of it.

She leaned her bicycle against the gate post – there was no fence left, so there was no point in the gate anyway – and walked round to the back door.

She lifted her hand, but the door opened before she could knock. Someone had been watching her from the window.

'Hullo,' Carol said. She looked like Rose had imagined her, lively, sharp, short curly brown hair.

'Hullo,' Rose said. They looked at each other. It was funny. Rose knew Carol, but Carol did not know Rose.

'I – er, can I come in?' Rose had planned that she must say what she had to say to as many members of the family as possible.

'What's it about?' Carol looked a bit nervous, as if she was used to people coming to the door for money owed.

'Who is it?' A yell from within, breaking on Mrs Morgan's cigarette cough.

'What's your name?'

'Isobel Forest.' Rose had always liked the queenly name of Isobel, and Forest was near enough to Wood.

'Come in or go out,' Mrs Morgan's voice said. 'There's a wicked draught.'

Carol stepped aside and Rose stepped in. Mrs Morgan was by the window in the armchair with the sagging seat, her bottom almost on the floor. Mavis was writing a letter at the table, with the remains of breakfast pushed aside. Davey was on the floor with a crust. Gregory came up to Rose with round trusting eyes, and said, ''Ull-'ull-'ullo.'

Rose crouched down to him, as Carol always did, to make herself his size. 'What's your name?'

'Gregory,' he said through his fingers, which were all crammed into his mouth.

'That's nice.' Davey crawled over to Rose and held out his chewed crust. 'And who are you?'

He couldn't or wouldn't say.

'Who have you come to see,' Mrs Morgan wanted to know, 'us or the babies? Are you someone from Carol's school?'

'No,' Rose and Carol said together.

'I live near here,' Rose said, 'and I was wondering if you'd seen my puppy. I lost him, you see.'

'Oh, poor you,' Carol said. Mrs Morgan tutted and shook her head sentimentally, and even Mavis looked up.

'What's he look like?' she asked.

'Little and brown, sort of rough-haired,' Rose invented. 'Only half a tail.'

'Why?'

'It got caught in a door when he was tiny.'

'Oh.' The family drew in their breath.

'I saw a black and white dog that looked lost,' Mavis said. 'Almost brought him home. But he had a long tail.'

Rose shook her head. 'That's not Mousy.'

'Mousy? That his name?'

'Because he's mouse-coloured. I dream about him every night. He's been gone four days.'

'Oh *dear*.'

Davey crawled over to her . . .

They were so nice and sympathetic that Rose felt bad about making it up, but she had to get on with the dreams. 'I dream a lot,' she said.

'Oh, so do I,' said Carol. 'Last night I dreamed I was in a film studio, and –'

'I see things in dreams sometimes.' Rose had to interrupt her, to get to the important part. 'As a matter of fact, I had a dream about this house.'

'What about it?' The mother leaned forward, looking a little less nice and more suspicious.

'Da– The little boy was here, and he was in danger,' Rose said quickly. There, it was said. She had thought they would be shocked or alarmed, but they all laughed, including Gregory, and then Davey, who liked to laugh, 'Ha-ha-ha-ha,' on one note, when the family laughed.

'Sometimes my dreams come true,' Rose persisted. 'Please be careful of him.'

'Come off it,' Mavis said. 'He's the most cared-for kid in the universe.'

'Apple of everyone's eye, he is.' His mother bent,

coughing, to pick him up, and hugged him, blowing cigarette smoke all over his face. 'No one's going to hurt a hair of his little head.'

'Well.' Rose did not know what else to say. 'I'm just telling you.'

'Thanks, but don't bother.' Carol edged her to the door. Behind her, she heard Mavis whisper to Mrs Morgan, 'What's wrong with her? Bit barmy, I'd say.'

'I hope you find Mousy,' Carol said as Rose went out.

'Thanks.'

Before the door closed, she heard them explode in laughter at the ridiculous idea that anything could happen to their precious Davey.

CHAPTER THIRTEEN

Rose's warning hadn't worked. What could she do now?

All the way home, frustrated from having failed to make the Morgans understand, Rose puzzled once more over the few clues that she had.

A child was in trouble, or danger. Was not in trouble now, since Davey was perfectly all right, so it must be something that was going to happen.

She knew the house, and where it was.

Mr Morgan was taking his family to a fun fair.

Gwendolyn had a date for her birthday. Where did she fit in? Was she a friend of the family? Was she going to the fun fair with them on her birthday? When was her birthday?

The fun fair was starting next week, Rose knew, but it would be there for several days. Was she supposed to go there every day and try to find the Morgans? Was she supposed to go to their house every day, in case something bad happened? They thought she was barmy already. They would have her arrested if she kept turning up.

It was all too much for her. This time, Favour, you've tried this poor messenger too hard. 'I'll do anything for you, *anything*,' she told him, lifting the front wheel of Old Paint to pretend it was the grey horse taking off, 'but I've got to know what it is I have to do.'

When Rose got back to the hotel, Ben was there. His father was going to rent a boat next summer, and he and Ben had come down to look at it.

'Been out running?' he asked, when Rose trudged in, flushed and tired from the ride back from Newcome.

'Out on my bike. It's on its last legs. I'm getting a new one, you know. Silver and white.' It was going to be called Great Grey Mare, as a compliment to Favour. 'They're

107

keeping it for me at the shop, and I may have enough to get it next week. So this is the swan song of poor Old Paint. I want him to have a few last flings with me in the evening of his days.'

'Going to have him put to sleep?'

'Or let him rust quietly away behind the shed by the twisted crab apple tree, in the garden he loved so well.'

Ben put his hand to his heart and bowed. 'He was a very gallant gentleman.'

That was one of the things that was different about Ben. Most boys didn't like that sort of talk.

'Listen.' He picked up the local paper from a table in the hall. 'There's a fun fair over at the horse show fields, the other side of Newcome.'

'Is it starting today?' It was a shock to hear him talk about it, after it had been part of the puzzle in her mind.

'This afternoon. Let's go there before I have to go back. Dad says he'll take us.'

'All right.' Perhaps Rose was meant to go to the fun fair today. Perhaps today was the day that all the Morgans were going. Perhaps fate or Favour had put it into Mr Kelly's mind to come and look at the boat this Sunday. 'Can we take Abigail? She's riding over to lunch.'

Jim Fisher had helped Abigail and Rose to fix up a small fenced enclosure round the open shed at the bottom of the garden, so that Crackers could stay there when Abigail was at the hotel. She was going to leave him there while they all went to the fun fair.

At the last minute, something happened.

Rose and Abigail had put a load of lunch plates into the dishwasher. When Rose switched it on, and it started its Niagara noise, she could hardly believe her ears. Favour's tune was rising through and above the roar and rush and racket of the antiquated machine, which was on its last legs, like Rose's bicycle.

What was she going to do? Mr Kelly was waiting on the

108

verandah to take them to the fun fair. She couldn't ask him, 'Please wait while I just run up to Noah's Bowl and back.' She could not explain to any of them. She would have to miss the fair. What excuse could she invent?

Looking out of the scullery window for inspiration outdoors, where it was always more easily found, she saw Crackers grazing contentedly in his little plot of orchard grass.

Thanks, Crackers, you're a life saver.

Rose went through to the verandah where Ben and Abigail were fitting in some pieces of the jigsaw puzzle a guest had started.

'Guess what?' Another phrase she had picked up from Abigail. 'Would you two mind terribly if I don't go with you?'

Abigail said without looking up, 'It's a free country,' but Ben looked up, with real disappointment in his nice, open face.

It gave Rose a pang like being stabbed through the heart to have to say, 'I'd really love to take Crackers out on my own for a bit. Would you mind, Ab?'

'Help yourself. You've been doing fine on him. Just take it easy.'

'Oh, I will. Oh thanks.'

Ben shrugged and said to his father, 'Let's go then,' and Rose tore herself away, drawn by the imperious tune and powerful force which no attachment in her life was strong enough to resist.

Since the unhappy jumping session at Joyce's stables, Abigail had let Rose ride her dun pony, to recover her confidence. She had given her a few tips, although Rose would never be a good rider, which was odd, considering how splendidly she rode Favour in his galloping flight.

They had been out on the moor a few times, with Abigail on her mother's big pony Cheese, and Rose knew that she should not let Crackers trot or canter too fast, because he was hard to stop when he got going.

But she was in a hurry now. The tune was still in her head. She had a sense of Favour waiting impatiently, tossing his lovely Arab head and striking sparks from the rock. She knew that she would have to plunge blindly down through the perils of the mist, and reach the bridge as quickly as possible.

Once through the wood, she turned right to skirt the walled sheep pasture, and trotted Crackers steadily across the moor, following the paths she knew so well, turning when she saw the cone-shaped hill. He crossed a stream neatly and she let him stride out fast up the slope beyond it. She was going to pull him in before they got to the top, but as she shortened her reins, a bird started up right under his feet. He jumped sideways like a cat, put his head down and took off with her down the slope on the other side.

It was rough and rocky, the bed of a dried-up stream, and Rose was terrified that he was going to stumble. She sat back and pulled on the reins. She tried shortening one rein to turn him. Nothing worked. She sat tight and tried to do what Abigail would tell her if she were there.

'Think positive,' Abigail always said, so Rose sat still and thought that at least she was getting there quickly, and there was rising ground ahead. She would be able to slow him down there.

At the end of his disorganized descent, Crackers felt so good that he put his head down even farther and bucked. Rose did not fall off, but she flopped forward, and went up the opposite slope clinging round the pony's neck.

Well done.

Whose voice in her head? It couldn't be her own, because she didn't think she was doing well at all. Mr Vingo? It didn't quite sound like a human voice. It was as unexplainable as the gentle force that helped her back into the saddle, so that she could gather up her reins and her wits and pull Crackers to a stop at the crest of the hill.

There was the bulky dark rock, solid and reassuring, as if it had been the voice of the rock that spoke to her. At the

110

edge of the thicket, she got off and had to commit the unpardonable sin of tying Crackers to a sapling by his reins. (Sorry, Abigail, sorry, Crackers, shan't be long). She pushed her way through the trees to where the white mist lay over the valley as if it really were the surface of the lake, and charged down through it, shouting, 'Out of my way, you devils!'

They laughed at her, as if she were a very small puppy yapping at a big man's heavy boot. It made her feel small and puny, but she shouted again and went on. Her throat and nose were full of mist and the acrid smoke of their fires. She coughed, and could not shout any more, but she was almost at the bottom now. She was out into the sunlight. The horse was there, and they were off. Sorry again, Crackers, but this is much easier than riding you.

Through the singing roar of the wind came a different kind of music, a tooting, whistling, cymbal-clashing, oom-pah-pah kind of music that grew louder as the flight of the horse descended. His speed and movement changed. He was going gently up and down and round and round. The music was the blaring steam organ of a roundabout. Favour was one of its horses. He wasn't Favour. He had become a wooden horse with gaping red mouth and nostrils in a high, staring head, and shiny dappled paint.

On his back, Rose had become someone else in torn shoes and a wide black skirt, holding on with grubby hands to the curved wooden mane and watching the fair ground revolve round her – people, faces, tents, caravans – through half-closed eyes, pretending she was riding a real horse.

So Rose was at the fun fair after all. But not as Rose, wandering round with Ben and Abigail and wishing she had more money to spend. She was this girl who climbed off the wooden horse when the roundabout slowed and stopped, and jumped down on to the trodden grass.

'Thanks, Vince.' She waved to the roundabout man above her.

'OK, Meggie. Free ride for you any time.'

Meggie went past some of the other rides and ducked under some wires and went round a big generator truck to walk between two rows of amusement stalls, waving and calling out to the people who worked there. She went towards the Hoopla stall, which stood by itself in the middle.

'Here we go, here we go, step right up here and try your luck! Three rings for 10p, don't be shy ladies and gents, three rings for 10p – win a lovely watch, all kinds of valuable gifts! Step right up and try your luck!'

The girl inside the Hoopla stall stopped shouting when Meggie came up, and said, 'Where the hell have you been?'

'On the roundabout. What's it to you?'

'Like a bloomin' kid, you are.' The older girl shook her head. 'Come in here while I go back to the van for a bit. I've got things to do.'

Meggie vaulted over the barrier and went inside among the assorted prizes, which stood on a big round table on stands of different levels and sizes. The other girl took off an apron with big pockets full of coins, and Meggie put it on and took up the stick that had a lot of wooden rings on it.

'Step right up!' she called to the people who were wandering by. 'Three rings for 10p, it's a gift! Try your luck, I say, step right up and try your luck!'

'You all right then, Meggie?' a thin man with a grey, unshaven face and hands that were as dirty as Meggie's were from handling coins, called over from the Roll-a-Ball booth nearby.

'Piece of cake.' Meggie tossed her head when she spoke. 'Not that much business, anyway.'

'What a lousy town.'

Rose wanted to tell them that most of the tourists were gone and that Newcome people ate large lunches on Sundays and then sat on the ends of their spines, sleeping or watching television, or both, and didn't go out until a bit later; but Meggie had been here before, and knew that.

'It'll wake up this evening, Dad. Keep smiling. You won't take their money if you look at 'em with that face like a dead codfish stranded at low tide.' Or, as Abigail would have put it, 'Think positive.'

And there was Abigail, strolling along through the sparse crowds, eating an ice lolly, her eyes going from side to side, missing nothing, grinning at everybody, creating her own good time, as she always seemed able to do. Rose looked her straight in the face through Meggie's sharp eyes, but there was no sign of recognition, except the general grin that was for everybody.

Abigail walked over to Roll-a-Ball, tried a few and got nothing, and laughed.

Meggie's father said, 'Have another go, now you've got the hang of it,' and Abigail laughed again and allowed him to persuade her.

Rose was looking beyond her down the strip that was lined with stalls and booths. She was looking for the Morgans. Beyond the stalls and booths, huge lighted wheels turned, and piston arms swung shuddering rocket cabs high into the air. The Dodg'em cars crashed together, the pennants at the top of the roundabout went round and round, and there was always someone new – the Morgans? – coming through the door at the top of the helter-skelter with their mouths open to begin screaming as the mat took off with them.

Behind and above everything rose the huge frame of the Loop. As each captive load – the Morgans? – rose to the top of the curve and plunged into the dive, you could hear the shrieks from here, above half a dozen different kinds of amplified music, and the shouts of the fairground people.

'Come on, don't be shy! Step right up, and try your luck!' Meggie tossed her head and threw out her quick-fire patter. 'Take your chance now while there's still room to throw – get the best prizes while they last!'

Rose spotted Ben, working his way methodically down the booths on one side. He picked up a rifle and aimed very carefully at the moving line of ducks, and Rose saw the shooting gallery woman reach up and hand him something small from a shelf.

At Roll-a-Ball, he won two magenta and silver balloons. He gave them to Abigail, and they both wandered over to the Hoopla, chatting and laughing, the helium balloons travelling over their heads like a banner.

Rose looked at Ben and Abigail with dreadful jealousy. Meggie looked at them with an optimistic commercial eye.

'There you are!' she called, as if she had been waiting for them. 'Just in time to win the gold watch. Only one watch given away tonight – and it could be *you*!'

She put her hands in the apron pockets and jingled the change invitingly. 'Three rings for 10p, miss.' She slid the rings off the stick and held them out to Abigail. 'Three for you, mister.'

Ben took them without looking. He was concentrating on one of the prizes, judging the angle and distance.

'You want the watch?' Abigail asked him. 'The stand looks as if it's too big for the ring to go over.'

'Now, now, now,' Meggie warned her. 'This is Carson and Sons Novelties.' They still called it by its name from her grandfather's time, even though now it was Carson and Daughters. 'Everything fair. Everything square. What you see is what you get.' Because if it's not so, Rose heard Meggie think to herself, the inspector will be along, measuring and nagging, and you lose a day's profits, like we did at Scarborough over the silver bowl, though if anyone thinks you could make a living actually giving away prizes like that, they must be daft.

'Not the watch,' Ben said. It probably wouldn't run more than a day.'

''Ere, 'ere, 'ere,' from Meggie.

'See the little horse up there?' He nodded at one of the horse figures with red saddles and bridles and feathers for mane and tail that usually the girls went for. 'I'm going to get that for Rose.'

114

'I'm going to get that for Rose.'

Rose's heart leaped up so abruptly that Meggie hiccuped.

'Oh, swell,' Abigail said. 'Good old Rose, I wish she was here. She should have come with us. She can ride that pony any day. She's crazy.'

'Raving mad.' Ben took a wooden ring in his hand, felt the size and weight of it, and got his balance. 'Like all girls your age.'

Meggie, who was about the same age, said, ''Ere, 'ere, 'ere,' automatically, although she was giving change to another customer, and Abigail nudged Ben off his balance.

He started again, missed the first time, set his jaw, swung, threw, and the hoop settled neatly over the little blue-grey horse.

Meggie was pleased. It didn't pay to have too many people winning, but the horses came cheap from Hong Kong, and people had to win some of the time, to keep them spending money.

Ben and Abigail tried a few more throws. Rose had stopped watching them. She was still looking for the Morgans. At last she saw some familiar figures among the small crowd at the ice cream van.

The Morgan family. They were dressed up a bit, the father in a bottle green jacket, the mother in a dress like a tent, wearing her teeth. Arthur quite flashy, Mavis with a new hairdo. Carol wore her same old clothes and led Gregory by the hand. They turned from the van, all licking cornets. Nobody was carrying Davey.

He must be toddling after them. *Don't lose him in the crowd, you fools!* The colour had gone out of the day. All the fairground lights were on, and there were more people now, strolling, jostling, carrying huge purple plush animals. This was no place to let go of the hand of a child that age.

The Morgans came towards the Hoopla, stopping at other stalls, not spending money, just watching the players, laughing, teasing each other, having a good time. Nobody looked round for the little boy. The truth of it broke on Rose with a fearful simplicity.

116

Davey was not with them.

This was why the horse had brought her here, to show her that they had left him at home. Alone? They would never do that. Perhaps with someone cruel or careless, who had abandoned him.

Carol and Mavis came up to the Hoopla stand and looked at the watches and the jewellery, and told each other, 'I'd like that,' and, 'I'd go for that.'

'Have a go then.' Meggie held out the stick and shook the rings at them. Mavis fished out a coin and took three throws that were wild enough to make Meggie take pity on her and give her a free ring.

'You chuck it.' Mavis gave it to Carol, who aimed at a small soft rabbit, and missed.

'Not that, stupid. The bracelet.'

'I wanted it for Davey.' As Carol turned away with Mavis, Rose heard her say, 'Poor little beggar. I wish we'd brought him.'

'He's much too young.'

'I hope he's all right. She's a bit daft, that Gwendolyn or whatever she calls herself.'

'At least she's cheap.'

Gwendolyn. So this was where she and her birthday fitted in. This was why she couldn't go out with gape-jawed Vernon. They're right, thought Rose grimly. She is daft. Could she possibly be cruel as well?

Meggie's sister came back and took the apron and the rings, and Meggie and Rose ducked out of the stall and ran towards the noise and music and the circling lights that made the fair seem more glamorous than it was. When the roundabout stopped, Meggie hopped on, and pushed a boy out of the way to dart for the horse she always rode, the dappled, rearing one to which Favour had brought Rose. The machine groaned. The whistles blew and tooted. The blank-eyed ladies on the front of the organ clashed their cymbals, and as the roundabout gathered speed, Rose was whirled off it, right out of the person of Meggie, through a brief spinning vacuum and straight into a familiar, fat, gyrating body. Gwen was swaying about in front of the television in the front room at the Morgan's house.

When the programme ended and the commercials came on, Gwen felt hungry. Her mind got the message from her stomach and turned slowly in the direction of the frying pan on Mrs Morgan's stove. Time for some chips. On the way to the kitchen, she lumbered upstairs to look at Davey, sweetly asleep in Carol's bed, his cheek flushed, his fine fair hair damp with the intensity of his sleeping. Gwen fell over a toy and stepped on the loose squeaking floorboard, but he did not wake.

'No trouble from you tonight.' Gwen chuckled and went down to create the small explosion that lit the gas burner under the big fryer, which was always full of oil and used over and over again.

She took one of the packets of frozen chips out of the refrigerator – there was not much else in there – and put it by the stove until the oil was hot enough. Meanwhile, with a shuddering crash, the opening music for the next programme started. *Red Hot Pepper!* Gwen's favourite programme. She hurried into the front room, to see the Red Hot singers and dancers hurling themselves about the screen in a frenzy of sound and whirling arms and legs and dazzling coloured lights.

'Red . . . Hot . . . *Pepper!* Ai-ai-ai! Gwen put her arms in the air and threw her fat body about

Get back to the kitchen! Rose was in agony. *The oil, for God's sake. The gas flame's up high and the oil will burn.*

Gwen was obsessed by the music. *The oil! The kitchen – fire!* There must be something Rose could do to make her remember. But Gwendolyn's mind didn't work as fast as that. The music and movement absorbed her, and as she turned, Rose was spun out of the scene with the music in her head and another, terrifying sound – the hiss and sizzle of burning oil.

* * *

118

She woke lying heavily on the moor, her limbs aching, as if she had been flung there. She lay stunned for a moment, too shocked to get up. She had left the scene too soon. The house was going to catch fire. It was too late to help.

She got up wearily and went over to Crackers, who was calmly choosing and chewing sapling leaves, since Rose had been gone for no time at all, as far as he was concerned.

She hooked the reins over her arm and started to lead him back to the hotel. She had no energy to mount and ride him back. Sadness fell over her like a grey cloak. Too late. She had failed. As she plodded on, with Crackers nudging her pockets and bumping her with his head, she looked at her watch. Five o'clock. Red . . . Hot . . . *Pepper*, said the dejected tread of her feet.

Red Hot Pepper! Of course. Sundays. But it didn't start until seven o'clock. She must have been seeing two hours into the future when she was Gwen. The programme had not even begun. Gwen hadn't lit the gas under the fryer. Nothing had happened yet.

Should she call the Fire Brigade from home? But the fire wouldn't have started by now. If she waited till seven, they might get there too late. How could they get there anyway when she didn't even know the name of the street?

Two hours. How could she get there in time? Favour – help me. Rose turned back, tugging Crackers, who wanted to go home. She tied him again and crashed through the undergrowth.

'Favour!' But there was no valley there. No mist. Only the lake, lapping gently at the gravelly shore, its surface ruffled by the evening wind.

'Favour!' she called the horse, but only the lake birds answered her, sadly, and the wind in the thicket of trees.

CHAPTER FOURTEEN

She must go by herself. With the challenge, her energy
returned. She struggled on to Crackers, hopping on one foot
while he whirled in circles, and rode him fast for home.

Ordinarily, she kept him cautiously to a trot and a slow
canter, but in this emergency she was able to let him stride
out, covering the ups and downs of the moor, plunging
into the hollows and charging up the hills. Because Rose
did not really care now who was in charge, she was relaxed
enough to be able to remain in charge of the pony. Because
she was thinking only that Davey was in danger, there was
no room for being afraid. Was this how a good rider felt all
the time?

She steered Crackers carefully down the last bushy slope,
trotted him briskly through the wood and turned him out in
his little paddock to roll off the sweat.

Joyce would have a fit, but Rose had always felt that
rolling was better than brushing, and the idea of Joyce and
her rules seemed as far away as if they were on Mars.

Old Paint was leaning against the crab apple tree. 'Don't
choose today to die.' She wheeled him across the lawn to the
drive and was just going to mount, when her father came
out of the hotel.

'Rose – I need you.'

'Sorry, Dad. I'm in a dreadful hurry.'

'Just for a moment. I need you to nip up to the store room
and find a box of old papers for me.'

'Can't you find it yourself? I –'

'I'm too tall to clamber about among all that junk. Where
are you going in such a hurry?'

'To Newcome.'

'Why?'

Rose was too distraught to invent a reason. 'Oh, I can't tell you. Dad – it's a secret, sort of, but it's important.'

'More important than me?' He sometimes said things like this, which made you cringe.

'No, of course not, but look – oh well.' She took her foot off the bicycle pedal. 'I'll do it.'

She hared up all the flights of stairs and up the last narrow stair to the attic, where she hunted frantically for the right box among dozens of boxes and bits of furniture and pictures and piles of old curtains. She was just going to hare back down again to say she couldn't find it, when she saw the right label. She dragged the heavy box over to the stair and backed down, letting it thump from step to step.

Her father was on the landing, asking her to do something else, but she pretended not to hear, and flew on downstairs.

She rode like a demon, with her head down and her legs driven by urgency. Newcome had never been so far away. Although she was riding as fast as Old Paint could travel, it seemed to take forever. Her legs were exhausted. The bike rattled and jounced her aching body. The back tyre was getting flatter. She stopped twice to pump it up, and the last time, she abandoned the bicycle on a patch of waste land and took off over a fence, across a yard and down an alley, taking short cuts wherever she could towards the brick wall of the railway embankment.

Her hands and knees were bruised and grazed. Her breathing was harsh and rough, as if her throat was closing. She stumbled once and fell. Tears came, and her crying was the sound of the child crying.

'I can't get there. I'll die in the attempt.'

She got up, and changed that to, 'If I die in the attempt, I'll get there,' and somehow she could run on. She did not know what she was going to find. She did not know if she was too late. She had broken her watch climbing over the fence, and it seemed like much more than two hours since she had last looked at it on the moor.

She took off over a fence . . .

Too late . . . too late . . . Her heart pounded. Her breath rasped in her throat like the smoke from the fires of the terrible savage soldiers who were somehow mixed up with their wicked Lord in this race against time, this desperate contest between hope and disaster. She passed the grocer's shop. Through a window in the next house, her attention was caught by a blaze of light from a television set, and the crash of music and drums and howl of voices that was the programme that had sent Gwendolyn from the kitchen to dance along with *Red Hot Pepper*.

Now! It was now! Gwen had lit the gas, and the oil was burning *now*! The smoke in Rose's throat could really be smoke. The crying of the child that tormented her imagination was the real sound of Davey crying. As she turned the corner and ran down the Morgans' derelict street, she heard the child wailing and choking.

'Mumma!' Davey cried, and choked on a sob. 'Mumma!'

'I'm coming!' Rose croaked with the last of her breath.

The back door of the house crashed open, and a wild-eyed, wild-haired figure, totally hysterical, ran out yelling, 'Fire!', stumbled round the house and ran past Rose, blindly screaming.

Then Rose was through the gateless gateway, past Carol's bicycle and fighting her way into the kitchen, which was full of smoke. Flames blazed in the frying pan and the curtains were on fire.

Upstairs, Davey was cowering in the bed, sobbing and choking and staring in terror at the smoke seeping up through the loose floorboards.

Rose grabbed him and went to the door. She looked back at the smoke and thought of Carol, and had to go back and bend down, still holding Davey, to lift the floorboard and rescue the poems. Smoke poured up into her face and a small tongue of flame licked along a beam and leaped for her as she grabbed the papers blindly, choking, thrust them in her pocket and struggled to her feet with Davey.

The child clung to her, coughing, choking her still more

with his clutch round her neck as they went down the stairs where the smoke was beginning to climb. Rose knew the front door would not open. It had to be the kitchen. The flames had already spread. At the doorway, she was knocked back by the acrid smoke. She turned her head towards the hall, took a deep gulp of air and charged through the dense smoke and the heat of the fire with her eyes shut, and somehow down the back steps to the yard and out into the street.

A woman was running across the road from the opposite house, and people were coming down the street. Rose thrust Davey at the astonished woman, and ran through the railway arch.

On the other side, she lay for a while exhausted on some dirty grass, coughing and retching, trying to recover her breath and her senses. As in a far-off dream, she heard the fire engines, faint, then growing louder. It was not until she was on her way back to find her bicycle, climbing over the railway line beyond the viaduct where it was on level ground, that she felt the pain in her hand and saw that she had burned it, rescuing the poems.

The bicycle was in the bushes where she had left it. Over by the railway embankment, the sky was full of smoke. She pumpled up the bicycle, and headed for home in the gathering dusk. She was totally exhausted, but totally at peace.

She had to stop three times to pump up Old Paint, which was difficult with a burned hand. She headed straight for her room when she got home at last.

She was lying on top of the bed, asleep in her clothes, when her mother came up.

Mollie never said things like, 'Where on earth have you been?' She said now, 'Oh, Rose, your poor face is filthy, and you shirt's torn. Did you fall off the bike?'

Rose nodded. Too much sympathy, and she might cry. Gently, Mollie unwrapped the towel Rose had wound round her hand, and drew in her breath.

'I burned it in the kitchen,' Rose said huskily, and started to cough. Her throat was still very sore.

'And caught a cold, going off on your bike so late without a sweater.' Mollie sat down on the bed and stroked her hair. 'Your hair is filthy too. I'll wash it for you later on, if you can stay awake.'

Rose was already asleep again when her mother came back with ointment and bandages, and a glass of milk and honey and a huge piece of Sunday cake, which she baked every week, and was her best. Rose opened her eyes and saw on the tray the little blue and grey Hoopla horse with the red saddle and bridle.

'Ben won that at the fun fair. He left it for you, and said he'd see you at half term.'

'Oh good.' Rose winced as Mollie turned her hand over.

'How did you burn it?' her mother asked.

'Hot saucepan handle. I'm so clumsy.'

'Hilda didn't tell me.'

'She wasn't there.'

'Poor Rose, you do sound hoarse.' As she bandaged the hand, Mollie said without looking at her, 'I know it's a secret time, the age you are now. It was for me. If you can't tell me things, that's all right. Just don't ever stop being my friend.'

'Never.'

Rose would have given anything to be able to tell her what she had done. No, not quite anything. Not the risk of losing the horse and her job as a messenger because she had betrayed the secret.

Next morning, Rose's throat was still sore, and she had to miss school. Her father had a day off, so she had lunch with him in their apartment upstairs, watching the local news on television.

'In Newcome yesterday evening, a serious fire partly destroyed a house in the North End, already marked for demolition.'

And there were the Morgans in the street with the wreck of the house behind them, one half of it a blackened ruin.

'I understand the baby was saved by a heroic rescuer.' The television news man thrust the microphone in front of Mrs Morgan, wearing her tent and holding Davey with a blanket wrapped round him.

'That's right.' Mrs Morgan looked stunned. The whole family looked as if they had been hit by a tornado. Carol appeared to have been crying. 'We was at the fun fair, see, and the police come to us,' her mother went on. 'I said, "Davey!" and wanted to faint away, but he said at once the child was rescued.'

'By the baby sitter?'

'Must have been, but Gwen's not been able to talk since, her gran says. The shock of it, see?'

'Well, thank God for a heroine,' the television man said heartily. 'But you've lost almost everything. How does that feel?' He held the microphone out to Carol, who looked as if she were going to cry again and said, 'I lost my bike.'

'And your home too, I'm afraid.'

Mr Morgan, his thin hair on end, his green jacket buttoned up wrong, pushed his face towards the microphone and grinned. 'Blessing in disguise,' he said. 'Now the Council will have to find us decent housing.'

'If you ask me,' Philip Wood said, as the picture changed, 'he probably put a match to the house himself.'

Rose did not argue the point. Behind the Morgans, in the smoke still rising from the house, his mane and tail part of the smoke, she had seen a vision of the Great Grey Horse. He looked at Rose. No one else would ever know that she was the heroine, but in his full grey eye she saw his pride in her.

And Mr Vingo knew. When Rose went downstairs later, he said to her, 'I saw it on the telly. I knew that it was you.' He picked up her burned hand carefully and planted a ceremonial kiss on the bandage. 'Well done, O Rose of all Roses. Were you afraid?'

She nodded. She had lost her voice.

'Rose of all the world.'

When her mother gave her the money for working at the wedding, although she had not really earned it because she had been a bridesmaid part of the time, and not even there part of the time, Rose bought her new bicycle. She did not feel sorry for Old Paint any more, because she knew what she was going to do with him.

She was uneasy about telephoning strangers, especially official ones, but she nerved herself to ring the Housing Department and ask them about the Morgans.

'I'd like to help them,' she explained. 'I heard that girl say she had lost her bike in the fire, and I have an old one – well, it works all right, and I'd like to give it to her.'

'How nice of you.'

'But I don't know where she is.'

'I believe they're in temporary housing. Why don't you bring the bicycle here, and the social worker will see that she gets it.'

So Rose got Jim Fisher to mend the slow puncture, and to take her and the bicycle in the van to the Housing Office. When they got there, she was scared to go in and have to explain to a receptionist, so Jim said he would do it.

As he picked up Old Paint to carry him up the steps of the office building, Rose hopped out of the van and ran to the pillar box and posted the envelope with the poems to Carol Morgan, at the address of the Housing Office.

Carol would never understand who could have rescued her treasured poems from the fire. But she could look on it as a miracle, if she liked.